The Thinking Spot

A sequel to *A Pearl for Kizzy*

Ed Bethune

©

ALSO BY ED BETHUNE

Jackhammered, A Life of Adventure

Gay Panic in the Ozarks

Anatomy of a Memoir

A Pearl for Kizzy

Celebration

This book is a work of fiction. Names, characters, businesses, organizations, places, events and incidents are the product of the author's imagination or are used fictitiously. Any resemblance to actual events, locales, or persons living or dead is coincidental.

Copyright ©2020 Ed Bethune

All rights reserved. Except as permitted under copyright laws, no part of this publication may be reproduced, distributed, or transmitted in any form by any means, or stored in a database or retrieval system, without the prior written permission of the author or publisher.

Cover photo: Willyambradberry/123RF

For lovers of God's world.

PREFACE

This novel is a sequel to *A Pearl for Kizzy*.

In that book, Kizzy, a spirited child, lives with her family on a one-room ramshackle houseboat in Big Pearl, Arkansas. They fish, dig for mussels, look for pearls, and sell the shells to the button factory. It is a crude life made harder by the Great Depression, natural disasters, and prejudice.

Photograph by Jack Delano, U. S. Farm Security Administration, 1940

At the onset of World War II, Kizzy befriends a young boy—a refugee from Nazi Germany—and a cultured young woman who encourages her to read and learn from Jane Austen's books.

Kizzy yearns for a better life, but as she comes of age her dream of getting off the river is threatened by the evil Bully Bigshot and his Eugenics Center, a corrupt outfit that wants to rid the world of "river rats" like her through abortion and "better breeding." And there is Cormac, the lascivious man Kizzy calls her "make-do-stepfather."

Since the publication of *A Pearl for Kizzy* in 2016, many people have asked what happened to Kizzy and Stefan and Birdie and the other characters they had come to love.

I resisted the calls for a sequel until I read reports that He Jiankui, a scientist in China, had used CRSPR technology to edit the human genome, a procedure disdained by most authorities. His work resulted in the birth of genetically altered twin girls in November 2018.

That event led me to wonder what Kizzy and others in the fictional town of Big Pearl, Arkansas would think about the Chinese babies. They suffered through the maniacal efforts of Bully Bigshot and his Eugenics Center to rid the world of undesirables. Then they watched the eugenics madness spread, metastasizing into the Holocaust under Hitler and the Nazis.

What would they think about "designer babies," the catchphrase given to babies born of edits to the human genome?

Wondering led me to write this sequel, *The Thinking Spot*. But before opening the book, readers should pause to consider the wickedness of eugenics.

In *A Pearl for Kizzy*, the villain Bully Bigshot spewed hatred. When the authorities brought him to justice, he said this:

"We should sterilize all the undesirables. The problem goes beyond the Supreme Court case that dealt with imbeciles. Through scientific planning and intervention here in Jasper County we are weeding out the ne'er-do-wells, the lazy, the infirm, and the homosexuals. We are doing it because these undesirables—and that includes the Jews and the niggers—are corrupting our race.

"The river rats are a good example. They breed like a bunch of rabbits and we wind up taking care of them at the poorhouse.

"This is what we've been doing at the Eugenics Center since it opened in 1932, and by God, I aim to keep doing it. The women we have encouraged to get abortions don't know what's good for them …"

Bully Bigshot was an extremist, but many upstanding Americans bought into the idea that the world would be a better place if certain undesirables were not allowed to reproduce. The Carnegie Institution, the Rockefeller Foundation and the Harriman railroad conglomerate used their great wealth to support eugenics. And United States Supreme Court

Justice Oliver Wendell Holmes wrote an opinion upholding a compulsory sterilization law, saying, *inter alia,* "It is better for all the world ... three generations of imbeciles are enough."

That was then.

Today, advocates of genetic engineering say there is nothing to worry about, that we are entering an era of "good eugenics." They give soothing assurances that man can improve humanity without making terrible mistakes or committing new atrocities.

Is that possible? Isn't that what the eugenicists said 75 years ago? Is it right or wrong? Who decides?

In this book a new cast of characters emerges to deal with these questions. Kizzy, now in her 90s, reappears, but the main protagonists are her granddaughter Cassie Davis and Cassie's lifelong friend, Carson Hamilton.

We put down mad dogs; we kill the wild, untamed ox; we use the knife on sick sheep to stop their infecting the flock; we destroy abnormal offspring at birth; children, too, if they are born weak or deformed, we drown. Yet this is not the work of anger, but of reason—to separate the sound from the worthless.

Roman philosopher Seneca

Eugenic goals are most likely to be attained under another name than eugenics.

Frederick Osborn

PART I—1997

"What we have done for ourselves alone dies with us; what we have done for others and the world remains and is immortal."

Albert Pike

1

Birdie

As our "Greatest Generation" marches off the screen, genetic scientists are claiming that they have found ways to improve humankind, and that such changes are inevitable.

What we do with this puzzling deluge of new technology, artificial intelligence and genetic engineering will determine our fate.

The people of Big Pearl, Arkansas were not concerned about such things on a beautiful fall day in 1997, but soon they would be.

***

The military funeral inched its way through the narrow streets of town. A color guard, a Marine Corps Band, and a platoon of troops in dress blues marched to the mournful cadence of muffled drums.

A caisson pulled by six white horses, three with riders mounted, rumbled along. Hushed words—murmurs of praise, sorrow, respect, and pride—added solemnity to the sound of clopping hooves, jangling tack, and the shuffling feet of the thousands who lined the parade route.

In the long black car following the caisson, Kizzy Halder pulled Cassie Davis, her 10-year-old granddaughter, so close that the child's auburn hair mingled with gray hair that had once been red.

Stefan Halder watched through tired eyes, marveling at the resemblance, thinking of that day in 1941when he first met Kizzy. She was a "river rat," living on the Black River in a ramshackle houseboat that had no plumbing or electricity, despised by well-to-do folks in Big Pearl. He nodded his approval. *Cassie's going to be taller, her hair's a shade darker, but she's the spitting image of Kizzy.*

As the procession passed the Big Pearl Library and Veterans Center, Kizzy and Cassie waived to a young soldier tending an empty wheelchair marked "In memory of Uncle Mac." Stefan tipped his cap in honor of the grizzled veteran who had meant so much to Kizzy during the hardest time of her life. Everyone called Uncle Mac the "smartest man in the county" because it was so.

The funeral for Corporal L. W. "Birdie" Barden, USMC, was the biggest event in Big Pearl since the last days of World War II when the townspeople turned out for a festive parade to honor him. Birdie—a poor river rat who overcame the odds—had been crippled in the fierce fighting on Peleliu Island. And for his heroism he received the nation's highest award for valor, the Medal of Honor.

Today, the people of Big Pearl honored him in death. Solemn but proud, they lined the parade route.

Little children waved American flags, some imitating the respectful hand salutes of veterans young and old.

An old work mule plodded oddly behind the caisson, led by a spindly little girl dressed in worn-out clothes. It was Birdie's only request, a reminder of the days when river rats like Kizzy and Birdie were treated as vermin, a poignant symbol shaming the arrogant townsfolk who had turned a blind eye to the horrors of Bully Bigshot and his Eugenics Center.

2

Tombstones

The caisson crunched across a pea-gravel drive that passed beneath the entry arch of Big Pearl Cemetery as the procession twisted its way through rows of gravestones. It neared the back side of the cemetery, the resting place for paupers.

There lay Shirley—Birdie's mother—who died at the hands of an abortionist, a victim of the eugenics craze that seized America in the years before and during WWII.

Birdie's young wife Olivia—who encouraged Kizzy to read Jane Austen and taught her how to be a lady—lay near Shirley.

As the troops took position, Kizzy pulled her sobbing granddaughter tight against her breast and pointed to a rough stone marker. "That's where we buried Grandpa, over there by the fence. Birdie was here that day, home from the CCC."

She thumbed toward the river. "MeeMaw isn't here, of course. We lost her in the Flood of '37."

Cassie had heard it all before, but Kizzy mumbled on, "My ma, Sarah, is over there with the others. The gravedigger called us 'charity cases' and said we had to take whatever was available."

As Cassie snuggled closer, Kizzy reminisced. *Shirley was like a mother to me. I hate it that she died so young, but when Birdie found out that the Eugenics Center was behind her death, he proved they did it and brought them down, and then he got me off for killing Cormac.*

When the funeral car stopped, her voice turned angry. "Bully Bigshot wanted to rid the world of people like us, but he went to prison and died there. ... It was a terrible time."

Kizzy looked skyward and sighed. *That's the short version. I've never told the worst of it—that Cormac was screwing me and tried to whore me out in Memphis. I'm taking that secret to the grave with me.*

***

When Kizzy, Stefan, and Cassie were seated the pallbearers, six enlisted Marines, gently pulled Birdie's flag-covered casket from the caisson and marched at the half-step to a gravesite between those of his wife and mother.

Directly across from the family, beyond the casket, a scrawny snaggle-toothed 10-year-old boy, Carson Hamilton, stood with his parents. His eyes were fixed on Cassie, but when she caught him looking, he blushed and looked away.

The preacher spoke for 20 minutes, telling how Birdie did his part in *two* wars: First he told the story of

15

Birdie's heroism with the Marines in the South Pacific, then how Birdie won what the preacher called "the war against the weak."

"Birdie brought down Bully Bigshot, an evil man who said he was trying to rid the world of 'niggers, Jews, and river rats.'"

Everyone flinched when the preacher spoke the words, but not a soul amongst the mourners thought them inappropriate.

He ended by saying Birdie never got the big head for being a Medal of Honor recipient. And when he said, "Rest in peace, good and faithful servant," the Marines fired a 21-gun salute and smartly folded the flag into a triangle—13 folds representing the 13 colonies—showing only the blue field with stars.

The Marine in charge gently placed the flag in Kizzy's hands and recited the familiar words: "On behalf of the President of the United States, the United States Marine Corps and a grateful Nation, please accept this flag as a symbol of our appreciation for your loved one's honorable and faithful service."

Just then, a nearby bugler played the haunting melody "Taps."

And as the last note drifted away, three sparrows swooped to a landing on Birdie's casket, breaking the silence with an unplanned concert. The little birds chirped a final song for their friend, the man who loved them.

Kizzy smiled, then sobbed along with Cassie.

3
"Chai"

Cassie's mother, Charlene Davis, did not attend Birdie's funeral.

She was in the hospital, suffering the last days of her life, the end of a four-year battle with breast cancer.

On the way home from the funeral Kizzy said, "Maybe we shouldn't visit your mother today. She's just too sick."

"But she told us to come after the funeral." Cassie sniffed. "And I want to see her!"

Kizzy looked her in the eye. "You're right, we should go. But let's take our cues from her."

***

Dr. Stefanie Bunswanger met them in the hallway outside Charlene's room. "She's having a fair day, all things considered."

"Can we go in?" Cassie begged.

The doctor nodded but pulled Kizzy aside. "Sometime in the next few days, I want to go over some family history with you. We've learned a lot lately about the causes of breast cancer. Some of it is good and some is not so good. Anyway, it's complicated and we can talk about it later, and there is no reason to hit Cassie with all this until she is older."

Cassie, ignoring the doctor-talk, pushed her way into the room.

When she saw her mother, she stopped cold. It was a familiar sight, but on this occasion the array of intravenous tubes and devices measuring her vitals signaled desperation.

Cassie moved to the foot of the bed and pulled the covers to the side. Her mother's leg was thin and cool as she lifted it, up and down, up and down, massaging her ankles and feet. The jumbled sound of the doctor and Kizzy talking seeped through the door, as did a burst of laughter from children passing by.

Cassie sobbed and put her head on her mother's lap. *First Birdie, now Mother. Who's next?*

***

Charlene, sensing her daughter's melancholy, managed to crack a tiny smile and gave her a cheerful greeting. "Hey, Cassie. I wish I could have been there for Birdie. He was my 'make-do uncle.'"

Kizzy entered the room in time to see that Charlene was trying to change the subject. She smoothed the tangles from Cassie's hair and said, "The whole thing was perfect. They put Birdie near Grandpa's grave, right between Olivia and Shirley. Everyone in town was there."

Charlene winked at Cassie. "More, tell me more."

"The Marines were elegant in their dress blues," Kizzy said.

Cassie stopped sniffling and told about the band and the bugler who played taps, but when she told about the sparrows that showed up to sing goodbye to Birdie, Charlene said, "That's where I want to be put, right there with our family, in the paupers' section."

Cassie broke down; her spell was back.

"Whoa now, Cassie, it's all right." Charlene winked at Kizzy and the child, labored to take a deep breath, then said, "Us people with river blood ain't afraid to talk about death and dying. Ain't that so, Kizzy?"

Kizzy put her arms around Cassie. "Yes, it's so. We've got to be brave. MeeMaw always said, 'it's the way of the river.'"

***

On Mother's Day 1998, a few weeks after Birdie's funeral, Charlene died. Scores of townsfolk joined Kizzy, Cassie, and Stefan for a Christian burial in a grave next to her husband, Charles Davis, who died in a car accident when Cassie was an infant.

Afterward, friends gathered to console the family and help themselves to endless plates of finger food, fried chicken, salads, and desserts. It was the Southern way, so Cassie stayed around to be courteous. But after a while she teared up and told Kizzy, "It's just too picknicky ... I'm going to my room."

***

Later, when everyone was gone, Kizzy and Stefan sat alone in the parlor, well away from Cassie's room.

Stefan said, "This has been a hard blow for her. She never knew her father and now her mother is gone. It reminds me of when my mother died from breast cancer."

They sat still for a while. Then Kizzy said, "I need to boost her spirits, so I've decided to give her this."

She pulled a golden pendant from her blouse. "You gave this to me when Bully Bigshot and his henchmen were trying to send me to prison for killing Cormac and I was low sick. It encouraged me and I think it will help her now."

Stefan nodded yes and with a finger traced the Hebrew letters on the pendant.

"Chai! The Hebrew letters show respect for 'Life and the Living God.' It helps us to understand that life goes on."

Kizzy said, "When I give it to her, I'm going to say exactly what you said when you gave it to me: 'There! Now you're safe. Enjoy every day of your life.'"

PART II—LEARNING

"Spoon-feeding in the long run teaches us nothing but the shape of the spoon."

E. M. Forster

4

High School

The brand-new Big Pearl High School bore little resemblance to the smallish school that Kizzy and Stefan attended in the 1940s. Tens of school districts were now consolidated into one, and children came from all parts of the county, feeding into town from every direction on yellow buses.

Still, lunchtime was the same. The kids who brought their lunches gathered outside when the weather was nice or in the gymnasium if it was cold or rainy.

Cassie and Carson Hamilton had been meeting for lunch since the third grade, when they were 8 years old.

As next-door neighbors they walked home together, then they would watch TV or play kids' games.

On January 26, 1998, when they were 10 years old, they were watching a favorite kids' show when a clip of the president burst onto the screen. He looked angry and wagged a crooked finger at viewers as if to make his point.

"I want to say one thing to the American people; I did not have sexual relations with that woman, Miss Lewinsky."

Cassie giggled. "What was that about?"

Carson said, "Sex." Then he shrugged and turned the TV to another channel, but the announcer on that station was also talking about the president's comment, so he turned the TV off and said, "Let's play checkers or Monopoly, or ..."

Cassie poked him in the ribs and grinned mischievously. "Let's play sex."

He froze when Cassie puckered her lips and leaned toward him.

Carson shied away, stuttering, "No. ... It's wrong."

They sat still, looking at each other.

Carson piddled with the checkerboard for a few seconds, then jumped up and ran home.

***

From that day forward the forays into sex continued as harmless play-acting—impish attempts by Cassie, pushbacks by Carson.

But they talked endlessly about everything else: Marriage, the kissing games other kids were playing, schoolwork, things like that.

Cassie was happy to have Carson as a trusted friend. His stable personality and faith in God were a perfect balance for her flighty, unbounded nature, and she seemed to know that. He knew how to settle her down and talk sense.

Then, on the day they graduated from middle school, Cassie tried again.

They were sitting on the couch at her house on a day when Kizzy and Stefan had gone to Memphis. Cassie poked her finger into Carson's chest for the umpteenth time, but this time she put her arms around him and whispered in his ear. "Let's do it, Carson. Let's play around. Just to experiment, that's all …"

Carson's recent flirtation with baritone gave way to the high and squeaky whine of his adolescence. "I can't, Cassie."

Cassie sighed and got up to leave the room, and when she got to the door she pirouetted, stood straight, and stiffened. Then she gave him the finger.

"Don't get mad, Cassie. We're just different. It's the way I was raised. … Don't go."

She grabbed the doorknob, but changed her mind and returned to the couch.

Carson said, "Some people say my mom and dad are old-fashioned, too religious, and I guess they are, but I love them, and I think they have a point. The preacher says it's wrong to play around until you are married. He calls it 'abstinence' and I've decided that I want to live that way."

***

After that Cassie said no more about abstinence, and neither did Carson.

But the dustup cleared the air, making them closer than ever. They had different beliefs, but they supported each other, and they had no secrets.

They made a dashing couple, the envy of their classmates, but the friendship was platonic, of necessity.

***

As they moved through the grades in senior high school, Carson earned a nickname that stuck. The boys started it, but the girls chimed in. He became "Rocky," a name derived from his outspoken Christian faith and the rock-solid physique and deep voice that blossomed in his sophomore year.

Carson was an even six feet tall with a chiseled face, perfect except for a conspicuous crook in his nose that listed to starboard, the result of catching a baseball pitch without a mask.

And he was popular, so much so that his fellow students elected him president of the senior class by acclamation.

***

Cassie matured in other ways.

Exceptionally bright, she excelled in every subject.

She was a live wire, a work-in-process, exploring life to the fullest just as her great-grandmother, MeeMaw, had done. For Cassie, the free-thinking ways of the river rats—bound only to the natural laws of the river—made sense.

She had the good looks and winsome shape of her grandmother, but unlike Kizzy she was curious and talkative in the extreme. Her mind raced from fad to fad, especially when it concerned cultural and political issues.

She respected Carson's faith, and his belief in abstinence, but thought it too confining. He was a good sounding board, but Cassie was restless.

She dated around, impatient to satisfy the mysterious urgings of her body.

Two senior boys were happy to help her in that regard, but for Cassie the intense secret sessions to learn about sex amounted to nothing more than youthful experimentation.

Carson figured out what she was doing. Cassie did not talk about it, but she made no effort to hide the escapades.

He cautioned her to slow down, but it did not take. She kept at it, saying it was part of her heritage as a river rat. "Church is all well and good, Carson, but my people have always lived free—it's the way of the river—and I don't see anything wrong with that."

***

One April Monday in 2005, late in their senior year at Big Pearl High School, Cassie and Carson met for lunch.

Carson slammed his Saint Louis Cardinal baseball cap on the lunch table, griping about what they were being taught in science classes. "Evolution is only a theory. God created the earth and made us in his image."

Kizzy ignored his rant. She had heard it before.

Her mind was on something else the biology teacher had said that day.

"He's talked about that before, Carson, but did you hear what he said about the discovery of a new gene that can cause breast cancer?"

Carson thought for a second, then said, "Lots of things cause cancer."

"I know, but my mom died of breast cancer, and I don't know if she had that BRCA gene. My grandmother always puts me off when I ask about it."

Carson said, "But if you tell her what you've learned today, I bet she'll open up. She probably just doesn't want to worry you about such stuff."

"I hope that's it, but I want to know."

***

That afternoon Cassie maneuvered Kizzy into the kitchen for a cup of coffee. At first, they joked about school, with Kizzy teasing Cassie about dating boys, especially Carson.

"He's just a good friend. I've known him forever."

Kizzy continued to tease, but Cassie stopped her.

"I learned something today at school about breast cancer that scares me. The teacher says they have learned about a certain gene that can cause breast cancer."

Kizzy pushed her chair back and frowned. "I know about the BRCA gene. The doctor told me about it when your mother died."

Cassie winced. "Do I have it?"

The world stopped spinning; all was quiet except for the ticking of an antique clock.

Kizzy smiled and shook her head no. "The doctors believe the cancer gene that killed Charlene was inherited from my husband's side of the family. Stefan's mother, Annemarie, died of breast cancer, but the doctors believe the BRCA gene that killed your mother most likely came from Stefan's biological father. His name was Victor and he died long ago in

Germany, in a farm accident. He was an Ashkenazi Jew and statistics show that they have a strong connection to the BRCA gene. We didn't know about any of that when you were born, but now we do."

Cassie squirmed and started to speak, but Kizzy held up her hand. "They're still learning about BRCA, but I asked if the gene might be buried in you and if you might somehow pass it on to a child of your own."

Cassie blinked, twisting the mother's ring Charlene had given her.

Kizzy touched her hand. "Dr. Bunswanger tested your blood and told me you *do not have* the gene."

Cassie sat still, stunned.

Then with a determined look that reminded Kizzy of MeeMaw, Cassie blurted out: "I'm going to learn all about this BRCA gene. And then I'm going to do something about it!"

***

Baccalaureate service for the graduating class of 2005 took place at the brand-new Civic Center in Big Pearl.

When the service was over Carson's mother grumbled. "It's just not the same. We used to hold baccalaureate in church, but the ACLU has pushed religion out of the picture. Religious liberty is supposed to mean that everybody is free to discuss religion, but these days it means hardly anybody can mention it."

An old man standing nearby nodded in agreement. "I graduated from Princeton. The baccalaureate services there used to be deeply religious. So much so that the sermons were broadcast over NBC radio." He shook his head. "But that all ended when the liberals took over."

Carson rolled his eyes. "It's just the way things are nowadays, Mother," he said as he turned his attention to Cassie, who was chatting up a cluster of squealing girls.

When Carson got Cassie's attention, she ran to him. "Can you believe it, Carson? We made it."

He gave her a hug. "God is good."

5
College

Cassie stood on the steps of Old Main on graduation day at Dearborn University amongst a cluster of chattering girlfriends, each telling their plans for life after undergraduate school.

Susie Blansett, who loved to crow about herself, looked straight at Cassie, who had not spoken. "How about you, Cassie?"

"I've decided to go to law school."

Susie screeched. "Law school! Why in the world would you do that? You majored in microbiology. The action is going to be in science."

Cassie said, "Maybe, maybe not. Anyway, I'm going to Montmartre Law School in Rhode Island."

Susie shook her head, mocking. "You're going to wind up handling divorce cases and doing mind-numbing research in the back room instead of working on the exciting stuff that's going on in the field of genetics."

Cassie gave her the small-eye, then looked at the others. "I like science, but there are lots of legal and ethical issues coming up. I've been reading about them. For example, there have been a lot of boo-boos made during *in vitro* fertilizations. Those are important lawsuits. There's a case in Los Angeles …"

The chattering started again; the girls had lost interest.

Cassie shrugged. "Those cases bother me, and I would rather work on them than to be a doctor or work in a research laboratory."

***

Seven months later, on December 18, 2009, Cassie finished her first exams at law school and headed home to Big Pearl for the holidays.

She met Carson on Sunday night for a stroll around town to see the Christmas decorations.

Cassie looked a little too fine for Big Pearl in her blue suede ankle boots and navy tailored coat with a matching tam that highlighted shoulder-length strands of auburn hair. The Ivy League getup looked extra-fancy next to Carson, who wore a rawhide jacket, beat-up jeans, a black cowboy hat and a slick pair of Tony Alamo roach-killer boots.

The little town hummed as the young and old strolled along, gathering in clusters to view window decorations put up by merchants trying to outdo each other with seasonal, mostly Christian displays. The ritual began during World War II when Kizzy worked at the library arranging displays of patriotic memorabilia collected from the families of those who had gone off to war.

A light snow started just as they got to the six big windows of the Big Pearl Library and Veterans Center.

Cassie tugged Carson's arm, pulling him toward the second window. "Look—Kizzy told me about this—they're showing the old-timey displays from World War II."

She pointed to an odd figure in the window. "There's a classic, the paper mâché of an old woman marching with a broomstick on her shoulder."

Carson laughed as he read aloud the sign the old woman carried: "I know I can't go, but I can let the boys know whose side I am on."

Cassie giggled. "Olivia—Birdie's wife—made that. ... She gave my grandmother Kizzy a job at the library and helped her get off the river. She doesn't talk much about her days as a river rat, but it was a hard life, real hard."

As they moved to the next window Cassie teared up. "Look, it's the display she made for the river rat boys who went off to war."

Two black and white photographs, one of Corporal L. W. "Birdie" Barden in his Marine Corps uniform, and another of his half-brothers in their Army attire, sat beneath a spotlight that highlighted a handwritten letter from Birdie to his mother. The envelope was postmarked Pearl Harbor, 1942.

The stuffed white dove that Birdie loved was perched next to a battered hand-carved boat paddle bearing a message in white cursive.

Cassie read it aloud. "The river boys are doing their part too."

Carson said, "It's hard for me to imagine how hard their life must have been. Fighting in the war, yes, but living down on the river. That must have been awful."

They stood at the window for a long time, then walked to a nearby coffee shop.

***

The Bumble Bee Coffee Shop was crowded, typical for a cold winter night. Cassie and Carson ordered their drinks and milled around talking to friends as they waited for three strangers to vacate their favorite booth.

Several friends from high school days kidded Carson about his new beard even though it was well trimmed, just a quarter-inch long.

He ignored them, but Cassie detected a smidgen of angst as the strangers vacated their booth.

As they sat down, Cassie grinned and punched him on the arm. "I like your beard. It's dark and matches your outfit. It's a perfect fit for the new you."

"I'm still the old me, Cassie. It's you that's changed."

Cassie grinned again. "I'll plead guilty to changing if you will."

They laughed, then unloaded, revealing as always, their innermost thoughts.

Carson told about his first year as an English teacher and coach.

"It was pretty much what I expected, but then I grew up with it—my parents have been in education forever. There's not much about being a teacher or a coach that I haven't heard."

"No disappointments?"

Carson hesitated. "Not really, but there is a teacher I'm not getting along with. He grew up in Big Pearl but went to school in California. He's been living and teaching in San Francisco for the last five years or so."

Carson massaged the whiskers on his chin. "He's weird … But otherwise, things are going OK. How about you?"

"Law school is good. I'm quite sure I made the right decision to go."

Carson said, "It surprised me when you passed on med school. You always said you wanted to learn more about genetics, breast cancer, and all that."

"Yes. But I learned about that by majoring in microbiology. The important action is going to be in the law."

Carson saw that she was itching to explain. "How so?"

He leaned back and sipped his coffee.

"Artificial intelligence—technology—genetic engineering!" Cassie swooshed her hand across the table to make her point. "It's all moving at lightning speed—exploding—as we speak."

Carson did a double-take, waiting for her next wave of energy.

"What are we going to do with all this knowledge?" Cassie said. "What *should* we do?"

She raised her voice. "Where is all this leading?"

Carson stared at her, then grinned.

"Stop it, Carson. These are *big* questions."

He gave her a serious look, then started giggling.

She wrinkled her brow and her face reddened. Then she giggled too, loud enough to attract attention.

When they composed themselves, Cassie leaned back in the booth. "Are you dating?" Her voice was casual, businesslike.

Carson hesitated, then nodded yes. "But I'm waiting for the right woman … you know that."

***

Later that night Cassie was home in her pajamas, helping Kizzy decorate a Christmas tree. It was the first time she had been home since starting law school, so Cassie bubbled as she told about what she was learning. She went through her classes, one by one, praising the professors, particularly those she described as progressive.

"College was enlightening, but law school is far out. I'm just a freshman but I can already see that I've made the right decision."

As they talked more and continued to decorate, Kizzy began placing the pieces of a nativity scene on the swirl of cotton beneath the lowest tree limbs. "I love these figurines—Stefan got them for me 20 years ago when he toured the Neander Valley in Germany, where he was born."

Cassie "They are pretty, but I like the secular ornaments best."

Kizzy winced. "But it's Christmas."

"I respect that, but virtually all my professors, in college and law school, teach a secular, more reasoned approach to life."

Kizzy grimaced but said nothing as she placed Baby Jesus in the manger and fiddled with the swaddling clothes. "There." She winked. "It is finished."

Cassie hung several candy canes on the tree, then sat beside Kizzy on the sofa.

As they admired their work, sipping cups of apple cider, Cassie said, "Carson and I walked downtown tonight to see the window decorations."

"Did you go to the library?"

"Yes! And guess what? They've brought back all the World War II decorations. We saw the letter from Birdie, the marching woman, and all that."

"Did they put out the old paddle? The one for the river rats?"

"Yep. It was there, telling how the river boys did their part."

Kizzy smiled and took a sip from her cup. "The world has changed, but so have I." She exhaled and her shoulders drooped.

Cassie settled back to let her grandmother reminisce about her days as a river rat.

"We used to dig mussels, looking for pearls; toe-digging we called it." Her eyes crinkled. "If we could just find a big pearl, we'd sell it and that would get us off the river."

"You found pearls, didn't you?"

"We found lots of little-bitty ones. We called them 'burying pearls' because they were big enough to pay for a no-frills burial, but not big enough to get us off the river."

Cassie touched Kizzy's wrinkled hand.

"It's OK, Cassie. I learned from an old man we called Knuckles that the pearl we all need to find isn't in the river."

Cassie knew the story but sat still as Kizzy told it again.

"Knuckles, a hermit who lived on the river, had spent years looking for riches but found God instead.

"I'll never forget the look in his eyes when he said, 'I done found my pearl.'"

Kizzy fondled her bracelet. "That's when I began my journey as a Christian."

Cassie leaned over to give her grandmother a warm hug. "I know you suffered under Bully Bigshot and with all the bad stuff that took place at the Eugenics Center, but things have changed."

Kizzy shook her head no, but Cassie persisted. "I know that some say we are doomed to repeat the mistakes of the past, but I don't believe that. This is going to be the era of 'good eugenics.'"

Kizzy scooted away from her and stiffened. "Let's talk about something else. … How's Carson? I saw him the other day and he looks good." She beamed. "Don't let him get away, Cassie."

"We'll be friends forever, but that's all." Cassie frowned. "He'll be a good catch for someone who's willing to live here in Big Pearl and put up with all the religious stuff."

PART III—WORKING

"The reasonable man adapts himself to the world: The unreasonable one persists in trying to adapt the world to himself. Therefore, all progress depends on the unreasonable man."

George Bernard Shaw

6

Carson

Baseball had always been the favorite sport in Big Pearl. The high school and local semi-pro teams used the same ballpark, one of the best in northeast Arkansas.

On May 30, 2012, the stands were buzzing, standing room only for the championship game; the Big Pearl Diggers—22-0 for the season—were heavy favorites to win over the twice-beaten Bolivar Lions.

Assistant Coach Carson Hamilton and Head Coach "Slats" Monroe had brought the team from the cellar to first place in three years, and they were leading 6-2 in the bottom of the ninth.

The Diggers' relief pitcher had the Lions on the ropes with two out, but the bases were full, and the cleanup hitter was at bat.

In the third row of seats along the third-base line sat Caesar Gastini, a frail man with stringy dirty-blond hair. He wore a green T-shirt bearing the dark image of Che Guevara.

Carson waved his arms wildly, encouraging the crowd to cheer louder, but as he turned to his right he spotted Caesar. *The weirdo! .... Here?*

He turned back to the playing field, took a quick look at Slats, and put his hands together, praying.

Slats nodded and signaled thumbs up just as Big Pearl's relief pitcher fired a curve ball, low and away, whiffing the batter to end the game.

The Diggers converged on the mound, surrounding the coaches, jumping up and down chanting, "We did it! We did it!"

Carson and Slats congratulated the boys. The celebration carried on for half an hour, but soon the stands were empty. The happy coaches gathered up the equipment, balls and bats, and headed for the Bumble Bee to critique their winning season.

It took the best part of an hour to review the game and the season, but when they finished and stood up to leave Slats asked Carson, out of the blue: "Are you and Cassie ever going to get together?"

"I don't know, Slats. She's changed …"

7

Cassie

The 2012 ceremony to swear in law school graduates who had passed the bar exam was held, as usual, in the courtroom in Memphis.

Carson was on the front row, seated beside Justin Bone, the managing partner of Barton, Bone and Dempsey, the Memphis law firm that Cassie had agreed to join.

Cassie, now 24 years old, smiled as the judge administered the oath.

And when the ceremony was over, Carson hugged her. "You're on your way now, Cassie. Congratulations."

Cassie grinned. "How about that! The first river rat from Big Pearl to make a lawyer."

***

Later that day, Carson and Cassie stood in the lobby of the Peabody Hotel, waiting for the afternoon march of the internationally famous Peabody Ducks.

At 5 p.m. sharp the tradition continued. Accompanied by John Philip Sousa's "King Cotton March," five mallards scrambled out of the elegant lobby fountain and marched across a red carpet on their way to the penthouse.

"I love stuff like this," Carson said as he pretended to march like the ducks, then they headed to the lobby bar for a drink.

***

"Here's to your new career." Carson said as they clinked glasses. "When do you start?"

"Tomorrow. I can't wait. …But what about you? How's life in Big Pearl?"

"I'm doing fine, but that guy I told you about—the one from San Francisco—is driving me crazy."

Cassie laughed. "You should have gone to school in the East with me."

"No thanks. One weirdo is plenty for me." Carson took a sip of his wine.
"But I want to hear about your new gig. What will you be doing? Have they told you yet?"

"I'm going to be working mostly with Jim Dempsey. He's the partner who works on health and science matters, mostly representing clients who want to patent new technologies."

"Sounds technical."

"It is, but Jim says I can help starting on Day One. He says they hired me because I majored in microbiology. Patent law is unique, but he says he'll teach me what I need to know about it."

Carson raised his glass "Well, if I know you, you'll be right there in the middle of it from the get-go."

"It's why I chose law school over med school. The action going forward is going to be in the field of law and ethics. It's fascinating. I've been interested in genetics forever."

"I know," he said. "But it's scary to think where all this is leading."

Cassie shook her head no. "I've heard that. Some are saying we are doomed to repeat the mistakes of the past, that all the talk of genetic engineering is just a new version of the old eugenics that rocked the country years ago—especially in Big Pearl—but I don't believe that."

"What about designer babies? I heard the science teachers at school arguing about it the other day." Carson said.

"I think we'll work through all that and that in the end it will be a good thing, the best of all possible worlds." Cassie said with a dreamy, idealistic look.

"Well, OK, 'Dr. Pangloss'—if you say so."

"Asshole."

Carson giggled. "I'm sorry, I couldn't resist it."

Cassie stamped her foot and turned her back to him. But then she began to giggle.

He put his arms around her, pulled her close and whispered in her ear. "I love you the most when you're like this."

Cassie turned around and kissed him. "You're a mystery, Carson."

***

Barton, Bone, and Dempsey—with 75 lawyers--had its main office in a high-rise on Second Street in downtown Memphis, just a few blocks from Beale Street, the "Home of the Blues." The firm also had satellite offices in Washington, D. C. and Nashville, Tennessee.

On her first day at work Cassie met everyone she could, particularly the support personnel who could make or break her career.

Jim Dempsey spent an hour familiarizing her with his cases before assigning her to summarize the latest cases before the United States Supreme Court that might affect his clients, particularly GENETECH or its CEO, Lacy Franklin.

***

Cassie buried herself in work for the next two weeks, staying late and starting early. On the day she finished the research project, Jim called her to his office.

Lacy Franklin, a debonair 33-year-old with a touch of widow-peak balding, got up from his chair to extend a friendly hand.

"Lacy, this is Cassie Davis, the brightest associate I've ever had."

"Jim tells me you will be working mainly on GENETECH matters."

"Yessir, Mr. Franklin."

Lacy chuckled. "Please. Just call me Lacy."

Jim said, "GENETECH is an up-and-coming genetic research firm headquartered right here in Memphis, Cassie. They have lots of questions, mostly due to the constant deluge of new regulations. Compliance is their main concern, so I've suggested to Lacy that you should be their first point of contact, and he has agreed."

"I'll do my best, Mr. Frank … er, Lacy."

Everyone laughed, including a slightly red-faced Cassie. Then they sat down to talk about the main concerns of GENETECH.

***

Cassie was proud to have her first client. She was also eager to explore the Beale Street music scene even though everyone at the firm cautioned that it was too touristy.

Even so, on Saturday night, she and another new associate went to the noisiest place on Beale Street to celebrate their good fortune as associates at Barton, Bone, and Dempsey.

The bar was crowded, but they squeezed in next to a couple of young men who had just ordered draft beers.

The tallest of the two—a tanned blond with a peach-fuzz beard—stared at Cassie, then he gave her a boyish smile and raised his mug of beer.

"Can I buy you a drink?"

"I don't even know you," she said.

"Sorry. I'm Chalkie. ... Chalkie Smothers."

By the time they finished their second beer the two had learned enough about each other to be comfortable. Chalkie, six foot two with a kind face, was a star first baseman for the Memphis Redbirds, a Triple-A farm team of the St. Louis Cardinals. The team had played a rare afternoon game that day that was won thanks to Chalkie's walk-off homer in the bottom of the ninth. He was very excited, he said; he was having a good year and expected to get to the majors before season's end.

By the time they finished their third beer the two were chit-chatting in the style of hip millennials, indicating their willingness to hook up.

***

On Sunday morning, Cassie slipped out of Chalkie's bed and tiptoed into the kitchen to make a pot of coffee.

She studied all his photos, news clippings and baseball memorabilia, satisfying herself that he was indeed destined for greater things.

Then she looked out the window at the Gothic church across the street. As the congregation, young and old, disappeared into the building, Cassie rubbed her chin.

Church is a big thing for Carson and my grands. ... I'll go to funerals and baccalaureates and things like that ... but the Christians need to loosen up.

8

Shakeup

In June of 2013, shortly after Cassie completed her first year at Barton, Bone, and Dempsey, the United States Supreme Court ruled that a naturally occurring DNA segment is a product of nature and not patent eligible merely because it has been isolated.

Jim and Lacy gathered in Jim's office to hear Cassie explain how the decision, *Association for Molecular Pathology v. Myriad Genetics*, invalidated patents on the BRCA1 and BRCA2 genes held by a GENETECHS competitor, Myriad Genetics.

She wound up her lawyer-like analysis of the case with the summary they were waiting to hear. "You cannot patent a 'product of nature.' … It's that simple."

Lacy slapped his leg and grinned. "Finally! The door is open for us to get in on the act. If we play our cards right the future of GENETECH is secure." He chuckled, "It won't make us as big as Amazon or Google. But the sky's the limit."

Cassie said, "Maybe, but a number of issues are cropping up that we'll have to deal with as we go forward."

Jim frowned. "So. It's not that simple after all?"

53

"Well, the court's decision *is* good for GENETECH. But there's more that we'll have to consider," she said.

"What, for instance?" Jim asked.

"Ever heard of Joe the Donor?"

Lacy laughed. "You mean the crazy son-of-a-bitch who offers to knock up women who are having a hard time getting pregnant?"

Cassie grinned, then got serious. "Yes. But Joe the Donor is just one example of how fast things are changing. There are lawsuits for wrongful birth and wrongful life. People are suing for mistakes made during *in vitro* fertilization. For example, a white woman is suing because her baby is black. … I could go on and on."

Jim looked at Lacy. "GENETECH will need to be extra-careful."

Lacy lowered his voice. "Let's just keep this—the negatives—to ourselves. I don't want to say or do anything that might scare off investors or frighten our employees."

9

Death

On February 14, 2014, Cassie called Carson to wish him a happy Valentine's Day and to celebrate the anniversary of their first meeting as next-door neighbors.

He said, "You never forget, do you?"

"You're my rock, Rocky."

"No. Noooo, Cassie. ... I've outgrown that moniker! ... *Finally!*"

She laughed, then quizzed him about his life as a teacher in Big Pearl. He gave low-key answers, claiming to be content.

Then—as was his way—Carson encouraged Cassie to talk about herself. It was easy.

"How's life at the firm?"

Cassie rambled for 10 minutes, telling how busy she had been, but focusing on several cases she had handled in municipal court.

"I thought you wanted to work on scientific stuff."

"I do, and I've been doing a lot of that for my main client, GENETECH. But the firm wants all new associates to get into the courtroom as soon as possible;

they say it'll make us better lawyers in the long run. And I've enjoyed that more than I thought I would."

Cassie did not mention her trysts with Chalkie, who had left Memphis at the end of the baseball season, or her latest beau, Ernie Blansett, a virile young lawyer who was clerking for a federal district judge.

***

A few weeks later, on Memorial Day, Stefan Halder collapsed while trimming the boxwoods he loved, the victim of a myocardial infarction. It was his third attack, a death sentence for the 86-year-old man.

The First United Methodist Church of Big Pearl was packed on June 3. Stefan's violin rested atop the silver-gray casket illuminated by a narrow ray of sunlight that seeped through the stained-glass window behind the altar.

All rose as the ushers led Kizzy and Cassie to the first pew. Carson followed, as did the members of The Gathering, Kizzy and Stefan's Sunday school class.

When everyone was seated and all was still, a young girl—Stefan's last student—cradled her violin to play Stefan's favorite: The Second Movement of Mendelssohn's Concerto in E minor.

The pastor eulogized Stefan, a child prodigy who escaped from Nazi Germany and passed up repeated offers to join The Philadelphia Symphony Orchestra.

"Stefan played occasionally with the Memphis Symphony, but he has taught scores of young people to play the violin and love music. His father taught him to play when he was barely big enough to hold a violin."

He pointed to the violin on the casket. "Yes, that violin.

"His journey, his love for Kizzy and Cassie and the people of Big Pearl is a beautiful story; one that is well-known to everyone who ever met Stefan.

"But Kizzy asked me to focus on a particular day in Stefan's youth because it tells as much about us as it does about him.

"Stefan was 8 years old, living in the Rhineland. His mother, a Christian, and his Jewish father wanted him to understand why they had to leave Germany. So they took him for a picnic to the nearby Neander Valley and told him how German laborers digging for limestone had found some old bones, remains the scientists later dubbed 'The Neanderthal Man.'"

The pastor noticed the puzzled looks, paused, then explained.

"Hitler, you see, was bastardizing the disciplines of archaeology and anthropology to support his ghastly theory of 'Aryan superiority.' He was not interested in truth, so he used phony information to stoke hatred for Jews and other 'undesirables.'

"Stefan told me last year that he still had nightmares about that day in the Neander Valley, the day he learned about prejudice and hatred.

"His parents had told him that Hitler hated Jews, but Aryans were OK.

"Stefan asked them, in the blunt way of children: 'Were the old bones Aryan or Jew?'

"Stefan remembered his father's answer, word for word: 'Well, nobody knows who they were or what they believed, but if someone says they were Jews the Nazis will not like the Neanderthal Man." The pastor paused for effect.

"From the mouths of babes. Isn't it an irony? This fine man who suffered the trauma of Nazi Germany wound up in a town that suffered similar prejudice in the days of Bully Bigshot and his terrible Eugenics Center.

"Today, as we say goodbye to Stefan, let's redouble the effort to love one another and make the most of our differences. We must not repeat the mistakes of the past."

A murmur filled the sanctuary as the pastor stepped back from the pulpit to a scattering of chants. "Amen, amen."

Kizzy and Cassie cried as the choir sang "Hear My Prayer" with its haunting verse: "O for the wings of a dove."

Cassie whispered to Carson, "Stefan loved Mendelssohn, especially this hymn."

***

One year later, on Independence Day 2015, Cassie drove home to visit 87-year-old Kizzy.

She noticed right away that Kizzy had a noticeable hitch in her step. "Are you OK? Are you sure you want to visit Grandfather's grave today?"

"It's just old age. Let's go. It's July the 4th and I need to put out his flag."

They picked up Carson on the way, and when they arrived Kizzy placed the small flag and a bouquet of red, white and blue mums by Stefan's headstone.

"My grandpa used to stand on the stern of our houseboat and make a speech every 4th of July about living on the river and how fortunate we were to be free."

Her lips parted as if to speak, but instead she bowed her head in prayer.

Lord, Stefan never met Grandpa, but he would have liked that speech. I pray that all my loved ones are together with you in Heaven.

Carson said, "Amen," but Cassie said nothing.

PART IV—SCIENCE

"When we try to pick out anything by itself we find it's hitched to everything else in the universe."

John Muir

10
CRSPR

"Congratulations, Cassie!" said an intern as he wheeled a three-drawer metal file cabinet into her new office.

Cassie pointed out the window. "How about that view of the Mississippi?"

"It fits. After all, you are now a Senior Counsel."

"Thanks, Malcolm."

Cassie's combined study of microbiology and law had put her in an exclusive category. She was one of the few lawyers in Memphis who could give good counsel on the tricky moral and ethical issues arising from the discovery of CRSPR, a technology that allows scientists to edit the human genome.

But it was the publicity she got for Barton, Bone, and Dempsey that resulted in the promotion and put her on the fast track to partner; with luck and hard work, she would make it in less than five years.

***

CRSPR baffled most lawyers, but not Cassie.

Beginning in her first year with the firm, she made it her business to learn everything she could about CRSPR. She read books, scientific papers, and attended high-level conferences dealing with gene editing, artificial intelligence, and the attendant ethical and moral consequences of CRSPR.

Thus, when CRSPR 9, a refined method for editing, made its appearance in 2013 she was ready. She took on several new clients who kept her busy, and Lacy put her to work writing guidelines, counseling employees, and critiquing their work to make sure that GENETECH followed the latest rules and regulations.

More and more prospective clients began asking for Cassie; the die was cast. She was on her way to another promotion.

***

In June of 2016, the *Memphis Star-Ledger* ran a big feature story in its Sunday edition with a spread of flattering photos portraying Cassie as *the* legal expert on matters involving genetic editing, particularly CRSPR 9.

A day later she was invited to speak to one of the largest Rotary Clubs in the South. Club members wanted to know where all this was headed.

On the first Monday of September 2016, she was at the head table in a room of 200 Rotarians, mostly men in business suits.

The club president gave an overlong, detailed account of Cassie's educational qualifications, reciting much of what had appeared in the newspaper a few months before.

Finally, he said, "My fellow Rotarians, I am pleased to introduce Miss Cassie Davis, a Senior Counsel at the prestigious firm of Barton, Bone, and Dempsey."

Cassie—about to give her first public speech—was hyperventilating as she placed her notes on the lectern. She needed something to break the tension, so she fumbled with her papers and spoke like a rube from the hills of Arkansas.

"Thankee, Mister President, but I'm thinkin' y'all may have over-egged the puddin' a little bit."

The audience gasped, then guffawed when they realized she was putting them on. Cassie's spell of hyperventilation vanished, and she gave a common-sense summary of the powerful gene editing tool, how it evolved, and what it might mean in the years to come.

When she finished, the Rotarians gave her a round of sustained applause, appreciating that she had made a complicated subject understandable and interesting.

Then she took several questions; the last was the hardest.

"Miss Davis, aren't we trying to take God's place with all this?"

Cassie said, "First, some perspective. Humans have been engineering genes for centuries. The vegetables and grains of today bear little resemblance to ancient crops. And the great variety of dogs proves man's intellect long before the advent of modern biology. Then in the 1970s scientists learned how to directly manipulate the genetic code stored in the cells of every living thing, but the technology was cumbersome and expensive.

"Then came CRISPR, allowing scientists to target, remove and replace any stretch of DNA in any living thing. It is easy, quick, and inexpensive.

"So, with all that in mind, let me say: You do have a point as to God's role in all this."

Cassie scratched her head and squinched her eyes. "Scary, isn't it?

"The speed with which our computers can learn has raised the prospect of what has been called 'Singularity'; that's a theory that we are headed for a time when artificial intelligence will bolt beyond us to create a world in which we—humans—are no longer masters.

"The answer to your question, therefore, depends upon who will win the epic struggle: God, Darwin, or the proponents of Singularity."

She nodded and stepped back. "Thanks for inviting me."

The stunned Rotarians gasped. But their clumsy moment of silence quickly gave way to hearty applause and the buzz of conversation.

***

The Board of Directors of GENETECH met 10 days after Cassie spoke to the Rotary Club.

Lacy and Cassie sat with six directors—men ranging in age from 29 to 55—to explore a variety of ways the company could make money in the new era of technology and genetic engineering. They were especially interested in CRSPR 9.

Lacy, as chair of the meeting, recognized Steve Love, the youngest director, who had a question for Cassie.

"What can GENETECH do? How far can we go with CRSPR?"

"Legally speaking: The sky's the limit. The regulatory authorities are way behind." Cassie shrugged her shoulders, then explained. "The laws differ from country to country and that is not likely to change.

"In the U.S., for instance, there is a hodgepodge of federal, state, and local laws that might apply. The FDA, for instance, has jurisdiction of some cases under the same authority it uses for *in vitro* fertilization.

"Even so, the enforcement of this new challenge is hard to predict. It would involve the politicians, the courts, and lobbying groups of all stripes. And those outcomes are often determined by emotion and public pressure.

65

"That's why most authorities say there should be a moratorium on heritable uses of CRSPR, but that hasn't happened yet.

"The World Health Organization is working on guidelines, but in the end, it will be up to scientists and companies like GENETECH to do the right thing."

Lacy said, "There's a fortune to be made, particularly for companies who can offer reliable gene editing to couples who want certain qualities in their babies. ..."

Cassie cut him off. "Whoa, we need to slow down. There's agreement right now that we should not get into editing the human genome. It's one thing to alter crops and animals, but almost everyone believes we should not tinker with human beings.

"There's too great a chance for error. The scientists who are editing with CRSPR 9 call such mistakes 'off-target edits,' but that's a euphemism. The truth is: Horrible mutations could occur, and those mistakes would be locked in; they would pass from generation to generation."

Lacy said, "But I read where some laboratories are already making do-it-yourself genetic engineering kits. One of them—admittedly run by a fanatic—says it is the way of the future. He says if government shuts people like him down that only the rich will be able to afford it and that will lead to the creation of two classes—those who have been perfected by genetic engineering and those who have not."

Cassie said, "Well, that's an extreme view, but it frames the issue. As your counsel I think GENETECH must stick with the majority view that draws a bright line between somatic editing and germline editing."

The board members wiggled around but said nothing.

Steve Love broke the silence. "Explain. What's the difference between somatic and germline?"

"Somatic editing is not heritable. Germline editing is. For example: If you edit genes to treat sickle-cell in a patient and do it in a way that does not pass from generation to generation, that's somatic. Germline editing, on the other hand, is editing that is heritable.

"And there is another distinction to keep in mind. Somatic editing is usually done as therapy, to treat a disease. Almost everyone supports *therapy* but opposes editing that is done solely for *enhancement*."

The directors conferred for an hour, then by a show of hands signaled the board's support for Cassie's advice.

Lacy said, "Let the record show that the somatic-germline distinction is the bright line that GENETECH will follow."

With that, the meeting ended, and every board member thanked Cassie for her good counsel.

***

At 10 p.m., Lacy drove to the Peabody Hotel and parked in the garage. He took the elevator to the lobby, and as soon as the doors opened, he spotted two men, one of whom appeared to be of Middle Eastern descent. They were sitting near the fountain sipping cups of tea.

Lacy put a finger to his lips, nodded to them and pointed upward, to the mezzanine.

The men did not speak to each other until they were seated in a secluded corner of the mezzanine.

Lacy shook hands with the older man, James Foster, who introduced him to 30-year-old Doctor Singh.

Lacy looked around, then spoke in a low voice. "OK, my board is now on record that we will follow the guidance of our counsel, Cassie Davis. GENETECH will not do germline editing.

"We are going to build a solid record of compliance, but in time someone, somewhere in the world is going to go over the line and make a designer baby. When that happens, the floodgates will open, and we need to be ready to make the most of the situation.

"So, let's talk about what you have done so far."

Foster smiled. "Things are going well. We have an option on a vacant resort that can be refitted. It's small, but big enough for a laboratory with all the necessary equipment, and several rooms for our customers … er, patients."

Foster motioned to the other man. "Dr. Singh is a skilled surgeon who has performed hundreds of *in vitro* procedures, and he is eager to moonlight for us. He has worked extensively with CRSPR 9 and—good news—if he runs into any unforeseen complications, he can always transfer patients to St. Joseph's Hospital where he practices.

"We're waiting for you to give us the green light."

Lacy said, "I'll give it, and release the funds we need, as soon as the genie is out of the bottle."

Foster and Dr. Singh grinned, rubbing their hands together.

Lacy smiled too, then got serious. "Gentlemen, if we do this right, we can make millions by giving wealthy people what they want, babies designed to their specifications."

11

Heritable

On November 26, 2016, Cassie took Kizzy to Sweetcheeks' Café in Big Pearl for Thanksgiving Day brunch. The old café, a working man's eatery overlooking the Black River, had been in business since well before World War II.

Sweetcheeks, the colorful matron who founded the restaurant, was gone, but the tantalizing smells were the same: Turkey and dressing with a wisp of pumpkin.

As they sat down Kizzy said, "I been coming here since I was a little girl … so many memories … some good, some not so good."

"That's why I wanted to come to this place." Cassie said. "I'm writing a book for lawyers about genetic engineering, the stuff I've been working on at the firm."

Kizzy touched Cassie's hand. "A book. That's impressive. I'm proud of you."

Cassie smiled, then in a serious tone, said, "I want to include a chapter about the eugenics craze that hit Big Pearl during the war years."

Kizzy blinked. "Hmmm. How much are you going to tell?"

"I'm not going to tell what happened to you personally, the trial and all that. I just want to tell about the Eugenics Center. The world needs to be reminded about all that."

Cassie pulled a sheet of paper from her purse and handed it to Kizzy. "That quote—something Bully Bigshot said—tells the story in a nutshell. And I want to put it in my book."

Kizzy mouthed Bully's words as she read to herself.

For years I tried to get those idiots in the Arkansas legislature to follow the lead of North Carolina and the other enlightened states that have passed compulsory sterilization laws.

Hell, I wanted them to go a step further. We should sterilize all the undesirables. The problem goes beyond the Supreme Court case that dealt with imbeciles. Through scientific planning and intervention here in Jasper County we are weeding out the ne'er-do-wells, the lazy, the infirm, and the homosexuals. We are doing it because these undesirables—and that includes the Jews and the niggers—are corrupting our race.

The river rats are a good example. They breed like a bunch of rabbits and we wind up taking care of them at the poorhouse.

This is what we've been doing at the Eugenics Center since it opened in 1932, and by God, I aim to keep doing it. The women we have encouraged to get abortions don't know what's good for them ...

Kizzy sighed and handed the paper back to Cassie. "It's a sad story that I don't like to think about, but it does need to be told—over and over again."

"I'm going to tell it!" Cassie looked Kizzy in the eye. "And I'm also going to tell how proud I am to be the granddaughter of a river rat."

***

Two weeks before Christmas in 2016, Cassie was in Lacy's office at GENETECH explaining a new FDA regulation.

When the meeting ended just before 5 p.m. Lacy said, "Let's go to the dog track in West Memphis; they have twilight racing."

Cassie hesitated. "I've never been, but OK. That sounds like fun."

Soon they were in Lacy's Lexus, and as they crossed the bridge into Arkansas Cassie said, "I'm writing a book about genetic engineering that will include a chapter about my heritage as an Arkansas river rat. Will you be one of my beta-readers?"

"A river rat?"

"Yep. And I'm proud of it."

"You're an interesting woman, Cassie."

As they entered Southland Racetrack Lacy put his arm around Cassie's waist and slid his hand lower with each step.

He said, "Let's watch a few races, and then I'd like to take you to the Pyramid for a special treat."

They lost the first three races, but Lacy hit a long-shot trifecta that paid $275.20.

And later that night they spent a luxurious evening at the Pyramid. Lacy had arranged massages and reserved a room with an incredible view of the Mississippi River.

It was her first fling with Lacy, but not her last.

***

Cassie finished the first draft of her book on February 21, 2017, and circulated it amongst the partners at Barton, Bone, and Dempsey.

Two weeks later, they gathered in the conference room to discuss how her work might be received by the public, and more importantly, the firm's clientele.

The partners were intrigued by the eugenics craze that struck Big Pearl but even more fascinated to learn about her grandmother's life on the river during the hard times of World War II.

Sam Barton, the senior partner, said, "I've studied the evils of the Holocaust, but what happened in America is hard to take. If we're not careful this new era of genetic engineering could turn into something just as awful."

Cassie said, "That thought has currency, but I'm convinced that this will be an era of good eugenics, not the evil that occurred under Bully Bigshot, who was a homegrown version of Hitler."

Jim Dempsey said, "But mistakes can be made with genetic engineering. Your draft points out that the science is not fully developed, that mutations—they call them off-target edits—can occur. Aren't you worried that by writing this book you will be regarded as an advocate for something that could go very wrong?"

Cassie said, "I make it very clear in the book that I stand with most authorities, including the World Health Organization and the National Institutes of Health: "Genetic editing should be used for somatic therapy, not germline enhancements. That's the bright line that will let us use this marvelous development for good, not evil."

"I hope you're right, Cassie," Sam Barton said. "But even if you are right there will be tons of litigation for the mistakes that will be made. I never thought I would live to see the day, but people are filing lawsuits for wrongful birth, and wrongful life."

Jim Dempsey said, "Yes, but imagine the horror of a designer baby with three legs or an extra head. … Cassie, you write in your draft that there is no way to prevent the creation of designer babies in some countries of the world. What's to keep this genie in the bottle, so to speak?"

Cassie pushed back. "Similar concerns were raised 30 years ago when *in vitro* fertilization was in its infancy. And guess what? Women *did* go to other countries to get it done.

"So, I can't say that designer babies will never happen, but we have to remember: A lot of good has already come from genetic engineering, sickle cell therapy to mention just one."

Charlie Bone, a partner who had not spoken, said. "I take Cassie's side on this. Furthermore, she has written a very good chapter that warns of an even greater challenge: The creation of two classes of people—the wealthy who have been perfected by genetic engineering, and the poor who have not."

Cassie said, "Exactly. Society must find a way to make the new technologies available to the masses, otherwise we could create a two-tiered society: The perfect and the useless.

"Oddly enough, it is the biohackers—the freelancers operating outside the established scientific community—who make the argument that the technology must be cheap and readily available to all. Their uncontrolled approach bothers me, but they have a point.

"And, finally, there are the transhumanists who say that all this is good and natural. They believe it will lead to a moment when man's inventions will take control of us humans."

The silence that followed her comment was broken by Sam Barton, who closed the meeting. "This is scary stuff, but Cassie's book will be a good thing for this firm, for her, and for humanity. God bless you for writing it."

***

For the next several months, Cassie busied herself making final edits to the book and dealing with a fast-growing caseload at the firm.

The weekends were saved for fun. She and Lacy would leave Memphis on Friday afternoon as early as they could get off and not return until late Sunday night. Their first getaway was to Mount Magazine in Arkansas where they hiked the trails, ate local delicacies, and—between episodes of torrid sex—enjoyed perfect vistas of the Arkansas River Valley.

They made similar road trips to Nashville, Tennessee, Cherokee Village, Arkansas, and Vicksburg, Mississippi.

***

In mid-June of 2017 they were planning to drive to Branson, Missouri for the weekend to enjoy a few musical performances, but Lacy called Cassie late Thursday morning to say that he could not go.

"I'm meeting some college buddies in Las Vegas. But I'll be back Sunday in time to have dinner at the Terrace at the River. I'll reserve that table you like, the one overlooking the river, for 8 p.m., if that works for you."

He let on that the trip was purely social, but it was not.

***

James Foster and Doctor Singh were waiting for Lacy in a quiet corner of the hotel lobby.

Lacy set his luggage down and they gathered around a low-lying table. Foster spoke first, giving a report of what he had accomplished, but soon the young doctor screeched, "I can't wait forever. I've got some debts that I need to take care of."

Lacy cleared his throat. "We've got to be patient. It's going to work out in time, but whoever designs the first baby will attract worldwide attention, and we don't want that."

The doctor drooped his head.

Lacy said, "Hold on, Doctor." He picked up a black duffel bag, set it on the table and inched it toward the doctor. "Foster told me you need a retainer, so here's $25,000 in cash to show we mean business."

Doctor Singh took the bag and shook Lacy's hand. "I understand." He nodded and smiled. "We have to wait for the dam to be broken."

***

Cassie wore a revealing purple dress for her Sunday evening rendezvous with Lacy at the Terrace at the River. Lacy was in the bar, waiting for her.

"How was Las Vegas?"

"Lacy chuckled. "My buddies never change, they just wanted to party. I wish I hadn't gone, but I've turned them down so many times … well, you know."

Cassie made a suspicious face. "It's OK, I get it. What happens in Vegas, stays in Vegas."

He laughed. "Let's get something to eat. I'm starved and I've got something for you."

They had dinner, and just before the dessert was served Lacy pulled a jewelry box from his jacket pocket and handed it to her.

He said, "Call it a down payment."

She opened the box. "It's beautiful, Lacy. It's must have cost a fortune," She put the glittering bracelet on her wrist.

He winked and took her hand. "You're worth it, and I'm hoping you will say yes when I give you the next bit of jewelry."

Cassie puckered her lips, then smiled.

And they left without touching their desserts.

PART V—QUESTIONS

"Fallacies do not cease to be fallacies because they become fashions."

G.K. Chesterton

12
Weird

On Tuesday, October 4, 2017, when Carson opened the door to his third-period English class, the students were not seated; they were gathered around his desk, and as soon as he stepped into the room they began to sing "Happy Birthday."

Then Sheila Mason, the senior class president, pointed to a large one-layer chocolate cake with 30 burning candles in the shape of a heart.

"You have to blow them out with one breath to get your wish, Mr. Hamilton."

Carson pretended to be making a wish, then laughed and took a deep breath to blow.

Sheila shouted, "All 30 of them."

The students howled, devoured the cake, and kidded him for being "ancient."

***

At noon that day in the school cafeteria Carson saw Sheila Mason again. She was having lunch with a half-dozen girls and they were fussing about something, but they stopped when he got close to wish him a happy birthday.

Carson said, "Thanks, but I seem to have interrupted an important debate."

The girls looked at one another, then yielded to Sheila.

"Oh, it's nothing, just something Mr. Gastini said in biology class this morning."

Carson shrugged and started to move away.

But Sheila's best friend, Mona Sampson, blurted out, "He said Darwin's theory is just the beginning. He says technology and artificial intelligence are going to change us into something entirely different from what we are. And he said we can't stop it …"

Mona whimpered and looked to Sheila, as did the other girls.

Sheila said, "You don't believe that, do you, Mr. Hamilton?"

Carson rubbed his chin, then smiled. "I believe we are created in God's image, and nothing Mr. Gastini says will ever change that."

Mona and the other girls nodded their approval.

And as Carson walked away, they began jabbering, talking over each other.

***

"He's half-crazy, Carson. Just let it go."

Carson had gone directly to the gym to tell Coach Slats Monroe what the girls had been talking about at lunch.

"If he's teaching crap like that somebody—the principal, or the school board—ought to do something about it."

"I wouldn't get into it if I were you. It's the old science versus religion thing. Anyway, Gastini is not a good fit for Big Pearl. I bet he'll gone at the end of this school year."

"I doubt that, but I'll keep my powder dry." Carson said.

***

A few weeks later, on Tuesday before Thanksgiving Day, Carson went to the teachers' lounge to get a cup of coffee and relax between classes.

Cesare Gastini, slouched in a chair, got up to leave as soon as he saw Carson. But he took a circuitous route through the lounge to stand close behind Carson who was pouring a touch of milk into his coffee.

"I hear you've been slandering me." Gastini said.

Carson turned to face him. "Truth is not slander, Gastini."

He pointed to the smaller man's tie. "Where's your Che Guevara shirt? If you're going to teach that progressive crap to the students, you ought to dress the part."

Gastini snarled, "Science is by nature progressive, dumbass."

The other teachers in the lounge, Carl Lofton and Mary Smothers, stopped what they were doing to watch as the argument intensified.

"It's not progressive to scare kids," Carson paused and put his face very close to Gastini's and raised his voice. "They tell me you've said that artificial intelligence is going to change us into something entirely different from what we are, that Darwin's theories are just the beginning."

"You actually know about Darwin?" Gastini cackled aloud. "I'm impressed."

Carson slammed a stiff finger into his chest, so hard that it backed him up a step "You need to shut the fuck up, Gastini, and go back to San Francisco."

Carl Lofton hurried over to get between them. "Whoa, fellas. That's enough."

13

Surprise

On Thanksgiving Day Cassie and Lacy had just sat down for an early-afternoon lunch at Paulette's, the elegant restaurant in the Harbor Town community on Mud Island just across Wolf River Harbor from the Pyramid.

They were sitting close together, talking in low tones, waiting for their entrée to be served when Cassie spotted Carson walking toward them with a pretty woman on his arm.

She flinched, then sat upright and waved to get his attention.

"Cassie." Carson hesitated. "What a nice surprise."

"I'll say." Cassie said as she stood up and moved around the table to give him a hug.

Carson chuckled and introduced his date, Marilyn Smythe. But the wrinkled look on his face did not fit the sound of his voice. "We're just two Big Pearl, Arkansas schoolteachers out for an afternoon in the big city."

Cassie noticed his odd manner but collected herself. "This is Lacy Franklin, he's the CEO of GENETECH, my No. 1 client."

Lacy shook Carson's hand and greeted Marilyn Smythe. Then he put his arm around Cassie's waist and pulled her close.

Carson winced as Cassie explained. "We've been dating for a while."

Lacy said, "Dating almost a year now. ... I've proposed. ... She hasn't said yes, but she hasn't said no either." He laughed. "I hope pretty soon that I can start introducing her as my fiancee."

Carson looked directly at Cassie, who searched for something to say but said nothing.

Marilyn broke the moment of clumsy silence. "Oh, that's wonderful. I wish you the best."

Cassie watched Carson as Marilyn spoke. *He's hurt. Surprised—bothered by the engagement talk—something's eating on him ... but I can't quite put my finger on it ...*

Carson said, "I wish you two the best." Then he looked at Cassie. "You know that."

As they walked away Lacy said something, but Cassie wasn't listening. She was watching Carson. *He's slumping, He's pissed about something, and it's not Lacy. Hmmm. It's not like him to be hostile, but I saw him like that a time or two when we were kids.*

86

14

Doubt

On Wednesday, two weeks before Christmas Day, Cassie had just settled into her apartment when her cellphone rang.

It was Kizzy. "Cassie, you need to come home. Carson is in trouble."

"Over what?"

"He got into a cuss-fight with another teacher. They were arguing about creation and all that. ... The school board says Carson is trying to teach religion in school."

"That's a no-no," Cassie said.

"I think they have put him on probation, but he told me that's not going to stop him. I've never seen him like this."

"Was his dust-up with that new teacher, the Gastini guy?"

"Yep."

***

On Friday night after work, Cassie drove to Big Pearl.

On Saturday morning Carson met her at Kizzy's house and told her the whole story: A blow-by-blow account of what he learned when he accidentally overheard the girls fussing in the cafeteria to his encounter with Gastini in the teacher's lounge. And, finally, he told her about a meeting he had with the principal, who put him on probation for cussing another teacher and advocating religion in public school.

Cassie just listened, waiting for him to wind down. Then she said, "The bottom line, Carson, is that you can't teach religion in a public school."

"I know that is the rule, but Gastini is going beyond Darwin. What he's teaching sounds like religion to me. So, what's good for the goose is good for the gander."

"That will be a hard sell, Carson. He will say that what he is teaching is science and the school board will most likely agree with him."

"I know. I know." Carson hung his head. "I shouldn't have lost my temper. I laid awake most of the night after we got into it, feeling ashamed of myself."

Cassie pulled him close, resting his head on her breasts. *I like the fight in him, that's a side of him I didn't know about. ...Hmmm ... That's what was eating on him when I saw him at Paulette's.*

He lay still for a moment, then sat upright. "Will you go to church with us tomorrow morning? Kizzy asked me to ask you."

Cassie hesitated, then nodded yes.

***

The Reverend David Orloff, the pastor who preached at Stefan's funeral, smiled when he saw Cassie sitting with Kizzy and Carson on the front row of the First United Methodist Church.

The choir sang "I'll Fly Away" as a prelude to the sermon. Their bouncy version generated a rowdy spirit, and when they sang the last note disjointed shouts of "Amen" filled the sanctuary.

The preacher took to the pulpit to give a sermon based on verses in the book of John. When he was sufficiently wound up, he left the pulpit to speak from the chancel rail. "In Him is the light of men, a light shining in the darkness. But the darkness does not comprehend it." He paused to let it sink in.

"Don't forget, my friends, that God is the creator of life, and Jesus Christ brings light to humankind. Let him guide you and you'll never need to stumble in darkness."

The preacher waited for nods of appreciation, then said, "Let me translate what this means to us in our daily lives." He looked directly at Cassie.

"Robert Frost wrote about two roads that diverge." He raised his arms to make a V.

"Those who just stand at the fork in the road are like a man with two watches; he's never quite sure what time it is.

"But if we choose the right road—the road that brings light to humankind—we will not stumble in the darkness. And, in that case, we'll be like a man with one watch; we will know what time it is.

**

That afternoon, just as Cassie was getting ready to head back to Memphis, Carson took her hand and nodded toward the living room.

"Can we talk some more? I've been thinking—fretting actually—about what the preacher said today."

Cassie sat on the couch and patted the spot next to her. "So, let's have it."

"I think I have to fight for what I think is right. The preacher said we need to choose the road that brings light to humankind. I shouldn't just stand at the fork in the road and keep my mouth shut."

Cassie said, "Gastini's got the upper hand, Carson. If you keep on, you'll get kicked out of school, and education is your life—just as it was for your parents."

"But what he's saying to the kids is pure malarkey. It's one thing to teach Darwin, I know I'd lose that fight. But he goes beyond that. He goes too far."

"You need to read my book, Carson. It touches on the school of thought that says man is constantly evolving and that one day—thanks to technology and artificial intelligence—humans will give way to an entirely new creation. They call it transhumanism."

"You don't believe that, do you, Cassie?"

"No, and I say as much in my book. But a lot of scientists do believe it and they present it as pure science, not religion. And that is why you will lose if you argue your point to the principal or the school board."

Carson stood up, looked out the window and clenched his fist. "I'll lose to those who have a secular worldview, but those who have a Christian worldview will agree with me. God doesn't want man screwing up *His* creation."

Cassie winced. *He has a point. There could be lots of mistakes—off-target edit ..., mutations—who knows what else could go wrong. ... No telling what evil people or governments might do with genetic engineering. ... shades of Bully Bigshot ...*

"It's wrong, Cassie, and I can't turn a blind eye to it. I'm going to fight Gastini and those who think like him."

He's boiling over. I need to back off, for now.

Carson faced her. "If the school board starts in on me, will you represent me?"

"Of course, but in the meantime don't do anything stupid."

15

Inquiry

On Monday morning, after Cassie returned to Memphis, she attended the regularly scheduled firm meeting for all lawyers. And when it was over, she started working on a backlog of cases that needed attention.

At 10:30 a.m., an assistant tapped on her door and peeked in.

"There's a man asking to see you."

"What does he want?"

"He wouldn't say, just that he had to speak to you privately."

***

Richard Rankin, a mid-30s man with a buttoned-down look, walked into her office. He introduced himself and Cassie pointed to a Queen Anne chair near her desk.

"What can I do for you?" She said.

"I'm with the Federal Drug Administration, but presently I'm assigned to the House Committee that is looking into the complicated issue of genetic engineering."

"So? Have you read my book?"

Rankin grinned. "Well, no. That's not what I'm here for." He leaned forward.

"We are looking into a tip from a confidential source that someone connected with GENETECH is planning to set up an offshore laboratory to create designer babies."

Cassie blinked.

"We don't have a subject identified at this time, but since you represent GENETECH we thought we should bring this information to you first."

Cassie said, "Do you have identification?"

Rankin showed her his credentials.

Cassie said, "Well, this is news to me. You must be mistaken because I know for a fact that GENETECH is firmly against germline editing."

Rankin said, "Our source cannot say it is GENETECH, only that someone connected with GENETECH is actively planning to set up a sort of do-it-yourself genetic engineering operation. They are planning to pitch it to wealthy people, saying that they can alter the human genome using the CRSPR 9 technique. They are promising people that they can control eye color, height, weight, and physique."

Cassie swallowed, but said nothing.

He continued. "They are exaggerating, saying that they can create higher intelligence, and fix certain cultural issues like work ethic and sexuality."

Cassie said, "That's bullshit. Someone is putting you on."

Rankin said, "Perhaps, perhaps not. We know that the science is not developed enough to make such claims, but we also know that unscrupulous people are chomping at the bit to take advantage of people who want to give their offspring every advantage."

Cassie said, "I expect there are extremists—biohackers—who will take advantage of people by promising miracles through CRSPR 9, but the science is not that reliable and may never be."

He said, "We are just getting started, but this is important because Congress is considering ways to control germline editing. The World Health Organization and many others want to draw a line to stop human genome editing. It's important work.

"Will you let me know if you hear of anything like what we have been told?"

Cassie said, "There are ethical limits to what I can say as an attorney for GENETECH, but I can assure you that the company is not planning anything like that. As their counsel I would know if they were."

***

Cassie stomped into Lacv's office at GENETECH that afternoon.

He was sitting behind his desk doing some paperwork.

"What the hell is going on, Lacy?"

He wrinkled his face, looking puzzled.

Cassie pointed to herself. "I had a visit today from an FDA inspector who is on assignment to the U. S. House of Representatives. He's investigating a tip they got that someone here is planning to get into the business of making designer babies."

"What did you tell him?" Lacy's puzzled look vanished.

Cassie said, "The truth. ... That GENETECH is firmly against germline gene editing."

"Good. That *is* the truth." He said.

"Yes, but when I said that he said, 'I didn't say it was the company. I said it was someone *from* GENETECH.'

Lacy mumbled, "He's just fishing."

"He said they—whoever *they* are—plan to make money by promising extravagant results. I told him there are extremists—biohackers—who may try to take advantage of people but, as counsel for GENETECH, I

96

©

assured him that we are not planning anything like that."

Lacy grinned and gave her a thumbs-up.

Cassie stared at him. *He's grinning, that's odd.*

She said, "You don't know anything about any of this, do you, Lacy?"

"Absolutely not, and I can't imagine anyone associated with the company would be planning such a thing."

Cassie gave him a second to say more, but he did not.

She said, "Well. … OK."

Cassie turned to leave, then stopped and looked at Lacy. "I know you are not as concerned as I am about where all the new technology is leading, but I don't want any part of anything that gets close to the kind of trouble we had in Big Pearl. … You know … the things I wrote about in my book."

"Not to worry, Cassie." Lacy said.

16

Creation

Carson donned his gym clothes and walked onto the basketball court where the team was doing agility drills, prepping for a big game. Carson loved the music of sports—barked commands, the occasional shriek of a whistle, the echo of squeaking shoes, moans and grunts—the unmistakable sights, sounds and smell of a basketball team hard at work.

He joined in to help and when practice was over, he sat down with Slats to talk about the upcoming game with the Newport Greyhounds, a feared rival.

Slats rattled nonstop, going over the scouting report and every detail of his game plan.

Suddenly he paused and looked at Carson, who said nothing.

Slats picked up where he left off. "They've got an exceptional guard, the Evans kid. He's fast as lightning. … He'll give us the most trouble. …"

Slats waved his hand in Carson's face. "Hello in there! … You haven't heard a word I've said."

"Sorry, Slats. I've been listening. I like the game plan. … It's just that I've got a lot going on right now."

"OK, let's have it. What's eatin' on you?"

"It's the weirdo. He's driving me nuts. ... You've heard me bitch about what he's teaching to the kids, but I can't get it off my mind. ... Cassie says I should read her book and study up on all the new stuff that's being taught in biology these days before I go off half-cocked."

Slats said. "So, if you study up you can go off fully-cocked?" He laughed at himself, then said, "Study up on biology? I'd rather take a whipping than to dissect frogs or learn about chromosomes and germs."

Carson smiled. "Amen to that, but she's saying I need to learn more about the stuff Gastini's talking about before I go off the deep end."

"Like what?"

"She says her book has a lot in it about where the scientists are headed with new technology and artificial intelligence. She says if that's what he's teaching then there's nothing I can do about it."

Slats said, "She's a smart woman."

Carson nodded. "She says I ought to stay out of it, but I don't think I can do that, Slats. And it's not just because I don't like the little shit, it's bigger than that."

"This is above my pay grade, Carson, but I know someone you might want to talk to."

"Who?"

"His name is Jonas Markham. He's involved with an outfit called The Religion and Science Syndicate. They call it RASS."

Carson said, "It's been illegal to teach creation science since the 1980s."

"I know, but Jonas says the world has changed a lot since then."

***

Cassie peeked at the ray of sunlight seeping through the blinds in Lacy's condo. *It must be close to 8 a.m. I've got to get going.*

She eased out of bed, trying not to wake Lacy. He was dead to the world, the result of an extra-long episode of lovemaking that kept them awake past midnight.

Her clothes were jumbled with his on a bedside chair and his blue blazer was on top of the pile.

When she picked up the blazer to put it on another chair, she saw something that was about to fall out of the inside pocket.

It was an out-of-date boarding pass. *Good grief, this is from last summer. Must be for the Las Vegas trip. ... But wait. ... This is for New York LaGuardia to Memphis. ...*

She opened her calendar and scrolled to the date on the boarding pass. *Just as I thought. That's the weekend he said he was in Las Vegas with his buddies.*

She left Lacy's place without waking him and called his administrative assistant. "Carol, I've been meaning to treat you to lunch for all the nice things you do to make my job easier. Can you meet me today at noon?"

***

That afternoon, when everyone but Lacy had left GENETECH, Cassie walked into his office. He was at his desk talking on the phone.

He waved for her to sit down but she stood, ramrod straight, waiting for him to finish.

"That was Clint McCormack." Lacy hung up and smiled. "He's going to sign the contract we sent over last week."

"You lied to me!" Cassie growled.

"What?"

"You didn't go to Las Vegas last June. You went to New York. What gives, Lacy?"

He did not answer. Instead he stood up and walked around his desk and tried to kiss her.

She pushed him away. "I'm not kidding, Lacy. I checked with Carol and she couldn't explain this."

She handed him the boarding pass from New York to Memphis that had his name on it.

He looked at it and hung his head.

"You lied to me and to Carol. She said she was sure you were going to Las Vegas to do some gambling because she saw you take some cash out of the safe."

Lacy started to speak, but Cassie interrupted him.

"You weren't meeting old college buddies, were you? Who did you meet in New York, and why did you need cash?"

Lacy said, "I can explain, but it'll take a while. Trust me, Cassie. Let's go over to the Peabody and get a drink, and if you are not too mad at me, we can stay for dinner and then go to my place."

"No. Explain it here, and now … if you can."

Lacy fumbled with his tie. "All right, I have been exploring the idea of an offshore organization to take advantage of the huge demand for designer babies. It would be separate from GENETECH, located in a place where such work is not prohibited by law. That's what the meeting in New York was about."

Cassie grimaced. "Legal or not, you are talking about germline genetic editing. That's wrong, morally and ethically. And, it's exactly opposite to the advice I have given you."

"You don't get it, do you, Cassie?" Lacy turned and looked out the window. "I am a transhumanist, committed to making humans better in every way."

He turned to face her. "We'll start with designer babies, but that's just the beginning."

Cassie, stunned, just looked at him. "So, who's in on this? Who did you meet in New York?"

Lacy stepped close and pointed to her face. "You don't need to know that, and I must remind you—counselor—that everything we have talked about is secret, protected by the lawyer-client privilege. Your lips are zipped!"

"Well … fuck you." Cassie wheeled and left his office.

17

Conflict

Carson sat across the table from a casually dressed elderly man and a middle-aged woman with a bouffant hairdo. Behind them on the wall was a huge cross surrounded by framed pictures of religious leaders teaching little children.

The man, Jonas Markham, said, "We started RASS, The Religion and Science Syndicate, in the early 1980s to support the law that was under siege. The critics said it was an unconstitutional attempt to promote religion. Unfortunately, the court stuck the law down, but we think you can help us reframe the issue."

Carson said, "I mainly want to stop one of the teachers at Big Pearl from teaching his own version of creation. And I'd rather not get involved in a legal brouhaha if that's possible."

The woman said, "I'm Claire Evans, Mr. Hamilton." She pointed to a thick file that lay in front of her. "That's the record from the case we lost. We have been looking for a way to restart our effort and we think your dispute with Cesare Gastini offers a unique opportunity."

"How so?" Carson said.

Jonas Markham said, "We want to argue that Gastini—who is a transhumanist—is not teaching science. The students tell us that he is teaching that humans will be completely redesigned, that technology and artificial intelligence will undo God's work"

Claire Evans said, "That is not science. That's religion."

Carson said, "So if he can teach religion, then so can I. Is that what you are saying?"

They both nodded yes, and Claire said, "Exactly!"

Jonas said, "We want you to openly teach creation science in your English class, and when you are challenged we will respond with a lawsuit that essentially says 'what's good for the goose, is good for the gander.'"

Carson pushed his chair away from the table and stood up. "I don't know. ... I'll have to think about it."

They stood and Claire said, "This new religion—transhumanism—is popular among the *nouveau riche* and the social engineers who seek the comforts and benefits of faith without recognizing God. They don't believe in the concepts of atonement or sin. Those are just 'inconveniences' to their way of thinking."

Jonas looked Carson in the eye. "It's preposterous, but it is their religion."

Claire said, "Please help us, Carson."

Carson rose early, made a pot of coffee, and sat down to review the notes he had made after his meeting with Jonas and Claire. Then he opened his laptop to do some last-minute research. At 8 a.m. he closed his computer, did some housekeeping, and left the house.

He started his old Ford Explorer and pulled out of the garage to begin the five-mile trip to Big Pearl High School.

Before he got to the end of the driveway he had to turn on the wipers to clear the windshield; a thick damp fog that had come with the morning. He could see no more than 50 feet, but when he got to the main road the fog lifted, giving way to a bank of low-lying gray clouds. He turned the radio to the sweet sound of Dolly Parton singing about a coat of many colors her mama made for her, but the dark clouds followed him all the way to school.

At 9 a.m. he trudged into his classroom, put his briefcase on the desk, and wrote several words on the chalkboard. When he put the chalk down, he looked outside through a bank of windows overlooking the street. He shook his head and shrugged when he saw a misshapen old man holding on to his hat, struggling to walk against the wind.

At 9:10 a.m. the students arrived for his senior English class, filling the room with a familiar buzz. He looked them over, the sparkling faces of youth, bright and hopeful even as they brought a scent of damp clothes and intriguing perfume.

He knocked on his desk to get order. "Today we are supposed to discuss creative writing, and I'll get to that, but first I have something to say about truth—what it is, and what it isn't. I know this is English class, but please bear with me."

Sheila Mason and Mona Sampson were on the front row—exactly where Carson asked them to sit—setting their phones to record his remarks.

He began with the bottom line. "I believe God created the world and everything in it.

"Mr. Gastini has been teaching a lie in his biology class."

Carson paused, looking for uneasiness. Some students squirmed, but he had their attention.

"When he teaches evolution, he says we are headed to a time when *homo sapiens*—humankind as we know it—will be replaced by an entirely new creature. He says this new being will be created by man, not God, through technology and artificial intelligence.

"Gastini says humans will engineer our DNA or otherwise harness medical science and technology to transcend normal physical limitations. And he promises that this will lead to an extended existence in this world, not the next—all this through wonders of applied science.

"This is called transhumanism. It is not truth. It is heresy."

He went to the chalkboard and raised a rollup screen to reveal the four points he had written earlier.

IT'S FOOLISH—To think man can replace God's creation with his own.

IT'S UNORTHODOX—Belies millennia of thought, study, and belief.

IT'S REPUGNANT—No telling what man's creation will be like.

IT DESTROYS DIGNITY OF MAN—They turn men into gods with the secular humanism that has infested our culture.

Mona raised her hand and Carson nodded to her.

"So, Mr. Gastini is saying man will replace God and create an entirely new being?"

"That's the size of it, Mona. Transhumanists think that will be a good thing. They say it is just another step to promote well-being, like what we are already doing with knee and hip replacements or genetic engineering to cure disease. They say if you believe those things are good, then you're already a little bit pregnant."

The boys in the class howled, and Mona blushed.

Carson shushed them and they settled down. "All kidding aside, Mona raises an important question.

There's a difference in using science to *improve* man. We are all for that. But the transhumanists go further; they dream of *enhancing* man to create a being that is entirely different from what we are now."

Mona broke a spell of stunned silence. "This is scary stuff."

Carson said, "I'll probably get in trouble for teaching about this, but I can't let Gastini go on with what he's doing. If he can teach his religion, I can teach mine."

Carson turned his back to the class, stuffed his notes into his briefcase and stormed out of the room.

The students looked at one another in wonderment. Then they got up to leave, buzzing about what they had just heard.

***

In the break between classes just before lunch, Carson stood in the hallway talking to Slats about an upcoming basketball game.

"Who do you think you are, Carson?' The screechy voice of Cesare Gastini was unmistakable.

Carson turned to face the smaller man, expecting an encounter.

Gastini said, "I hear you criticized what I teach in biology in your English class. That proves what a joke you are. You don't know dick about science or much of anything else."

"You don't belong here, Gastini. Go back to San Francisco where you fit in."

The two got face to face, pushing and shoving, but the spectacle ended when the students began to gather.

Gastini walked away first with a parting shot. "You'll pay for this, Pretty Boy. You don't know what you're getting into, and who you're messing with."

***

Cassie arrived in Big Pearl late that afternoon and went directly to Carson's place.

He was in his living room when she barged through the front door. "What were you thinking? The last thing I said to you was 'don't do anything stupid.'"

"I know." He gave her a sheepish look. "But I read what you wrote in your book about transhumanism, and I've done some other research."

"You'll need that and more to get out of this," Cassie said.

***

When Cassie stepped through the door of the principal's office at Big Pearl High School, memories of her high school days returned. She had been called there on several occasions to resolve an array of spurious accusations, mostly from kids who envied her academic prowess.

Joe Caldwell, now in his 22nd year as principal, had not changed a thing in his office except to mount the smiling photographs of currently serving political leaders. The old stuffed bobcat was still to the right of his desk, appearing to chase the overly fat raccoon. A weathered King James Bible lay on the corner of his mahogany desk, looking as if it had not been opened since her schooldays.

He greeted Cassie with his trademark look, a dour countenance that revealed nothing.

Cassie said hello and as they sat down, she looked for a glimmer of cheer, but it did not come.

"Thanks for seeing me, Mr. Caldwell. I want to discuss the trouble between Carson and Cesare Gastini."

"Carson knows better than to teach religion in school, Cassie."

"He says Gastini is doing the same thing. He says he has gone way beyond Darwin's theories to preach the religion of transhumanism."

"The members of the school board don't see it that way, Cassie. They think Gastini is just trying to tell the students where all the new technologies will lead."

Cassie shook her head and raised her voice. "Some students are saying Gastini really gets carried away when he talks about futuristic stuff. And that's the main problem with transhumanism."

Caldwell shook his head. "Gastini has his backers too, Cassie. The science teachers are in his corner."

Cassie started to speak, but Caldwell cut her off. "Carson cannot teach religion in public school, Cassie. That was decided years ago."

"I'll tell him that, but Carson has met with a group called The Religion and Science Syndicate. They are 100 percent behind him, saying they intend to resurrect the creation issue."

Caldwell said, "Well, Gastini has strong support that goes beyond our science teachers. There is a group called The Advocates for Science and Reason. They are threatening to take the school board to court if we don't stop Carson."

"I've heard of them. It's an extremist group. The media calls them TASAR and they have raised holy hell all across the country, often threatening violence to make their point."

"We don't need this in Big Pearl, Cassie. … Please do what you can to talk Carson off his high horse. If you'll promise to do that, I'll get the school board to hold off. After all, no one was hurt in the hallway skirmish that Carson and Gastini got into."

Cassie said, "I'll tell him what you said."

But as she left, other thoughts crossed her mind. *Carson's not going to pull back. In the old days he would have fallen in line to avoid conflict. But now he's on fire, determined to fight. Gastini is like a red flag, but there's more to it than that ... He's different from Lacy in so many ways. ... I wish I had seen that before now ...*

18

Earth-shaking

Cassie, as requested, stepped into the office of Sam Barton, the senior partner of Barton, Bone, and Dempsey at 10 a.m. sharp.

The rich mahogany walls were meant to give clients a sense of confidence and trust, but that is not what Cassie felt when she saw all three name-partners seated around a small conference table.

The managing partner, Justin Bone, spoke first. "Cassie, this is the first time in three years that we have had any reason to doubt your competence or commitment, but Lacy Franklin has instructed us to take you off of all GENETECH work."

Cassie looked directly at Jim Dempsey. "You assigned me to the GENETECH work when I first got here, and I have done a good job for the company. So much so that you all promoted me to Senior Counsel."

Dempsey said, "That's true, but Lacy won't take no for an answer."

"Did he tell you why he doesn't want me to do GENETECH work?"

Dempsey looked to Sam Barton, who said, "We know you have been dating Lacy for some time so I'm guessing you all have had a falling out of some sort."

Cassie laughed. "That's partly true, but there's more to it than that. Lacy is planning to set up a full-service clinic to make 'designer babies.'

"An FDA investigator who is assigned to a congressional committee came to see me. They are looking into it.

"You all know from reviewing my book that I believe it is morally wrong to genetically engineer the human genome. I told Lacy what the FDA man said but he shrugged it off. He says he is planning to do it in a country where it is legal."

Sam Barton said, "We are lawyers, Cassie, and it is our business to give legal advice. We should not make moral judgments about our clients."

Cassie said, "I know, but …"

Barton stood up and grumbled, "GENETECH is our best client. We get 40 percent of our fee income from Lacy's company. If he wants you off the case, you are off, and that's that."

The other partners stood up. Barton started talking to Dempsey, ignoring Cassie.

She headed for the door, and Justin Bone followed her into the hall.

"As managing partner, Cassie, I must tell you that we also think you are spending entirely too much time

115

in Big Pearl working *pro bono* on a controversial issue that you are sure to lose."

"Carson Hamilton is my best friend. He may be wrong, legally, but he is a good man and I mean to keep helping him."

***

A surprise late freeze came to Big Pearl in the wee hours of Sunday, March 11, 2018.

Kizzy got up at first light to check on the tender seedlings she had planted the day before. She pulled her robe tight and headed into the garden. A bluebird—on his way to fetch nest-makings—distracted her, sailing so close to her head that she lost her footing.

Kizzy put her hand down to break the fall but crashed hard to the ground. She struggled to get up and discovered that her right arm—lacking the muscle of youth—was useless, hanging limp by her side.

Stan Howard, her longtime neighbor, was just pulling out of his driveway when Kizzy got to her feet. She called to him and within minutes he had her in his pickup on the way to the Big Pearl Hospital.

***

Cassie was sound asleep when Kizzy called.

"Cassie, I'm OK, but I slipped on some ice this morning and broke my arm. The doctor patched me up and I'm home now having a cup of coffee with Carson."

Cassie said, "Are you sure you're all right?"

"Yes. I'm fine, except for feeling stupid. ... I've had some real adventures in my 90 years, but I've never broken anything 'til now," Kizzy whimpered. "Just lucky I guess."

Cassie said, "Do you want me to come home?"

When Kizzy did not respond, Cassie said, "I'll get dressed and be there in a couple of hours. Now let me talk to Carson."

Kizzy handed the phone to Carson. "She wants to talk to you."

Cassie said, "Thanks, Carson. You've always been there for me and for Kizzy." She spoke softly into the phone. "I've been worried about her for some time. You know what I mean. Whether she can take care of herself, and all that."

Carson said, "I'll stay with her until you get here."

***

For the next eight months Cassie spent every weekend in Big Pearl, leaving work as soon as she could, returning to Memphis as late as she could.

Cassie and Carson urged Kizzy to move into Revelation Senior Living, a sparkling new facility for seniors, but she would have none of it.

They tried for months, using every argument in the book. But Kizzy never wavered. Her endless array of creative objections always ended with an irrefutable declaration.

"Stefan and I built this house 60 years ago. He died here, and—Lord willing—this is where I'll be when I take my last breath."

Meanwhile, Cassie interviewed with several other Memphis law firms but could not find what she wanted. One firm was heavy into maritime law, another was mainly interested in representing farmers. Barton, Bone, and Dempsey was the best firm in Memphis for clients needing counsel on scientific issues, especially those dealing with genetic engineering.

Cassie was making a good salary, so she stayed, doing research, taking depositions, and handling minor litigation. She did not want to restart the personal relationship she had with Lacy but hoped she might once again be asked to do work for GENETECH.

***

On November 22, 2018, Cassie and Carson celebrated Thanksgiving Day with Kizzy, who spent the entire morning chirping around in the kitchen fixing her favorite dishes.

Carson and Cassie waited in the living room at Kizzy's insistence. She liked to cook on her own, and besides, she now trusted them to talk about something other than putting her into what she called "the old folks' home."

Cassie looked at Carson. "How're things at school?"

"Fine, I guess. I've been teaching English and avoiding Gastini.'

"Not talking about religion, I hope?"

"No, the Religion and Science Syndicate thinks we should lay low and not raise the issue again until something happens that might open the eyes of the public."

"Like what?"

"I don't know."

PART VI—FISSURE

"The bigger the dam of patience, the worse the flood when the dam breaks."

Austin O'Malley

19

Shock

On Monday, November 26, 2018, a headline in *The New York Times* shocked the world: "Chinese Scientist Claims to Use CRSPR To Make First Genetically Edited Babies."

The story was picked up by newspapers across the globe including the *Memphis Star-Ledger,* which ran it above the fold with a headline that stretched across the page. The Memphis paper ran an editorial the following day saying whoever was responsible for genetically engineering the birth of human babies should be punished for committing "a dastardly feat that could open the door to 'designer babies.'"

National leaders in the scientific and medical community also condemned the births, saying it was a misuse of the new CRSPR 9 technology. The Chinese scientist claimed that he genetically edited the babies to protect them from the HIV virus, but that was doubted.

Not to be outdone, U. S. politicians chimed in, sanctimoniously promising to fix the problem of "designer babies" even though there was already language in funding bills to prohibit the Food and Drug Administration from considering any application to create genetically modified human beings.

The publicity that followed set off a chain reaction, particularly in the scientific community. The majority railed against the Chinese scientist who engineered the babies and called for a strong moratorium, but a minority said that would be like taking a meat axe to a problem that cried out for a more subtle policy.

The battle lines soon took shape. The World Health Organization and the National Institute of Health came out against such practices.

Cassie was furious when she saw the story, but not surprised. The birth of the Chinese babies crossed the sharp line she drew in her book and public speeches defining the moral and ethical limits of human genome editing.

Later that day she made it a point to confront the partners at Barton, Bone, and Dempsey. She said the same thing to each of them: "I told you so."

That afternoon as she was driving home, she tuned to a radio talk show. The host was interviewing a radical transhumanist about the Chinese babies.

The guest, a leader of the TASAR group, said, "It's a good thing. We believe this is just the first step. Designer babies will give us better, smarter, healthier people. The process will flourish because people want their children to be healthy, smart, and have every advantage that science can give them. What's wrong with that? It's inevitable, just another step in an evolutionary process that is controlled by man, not God."

Cassie shook her head. *That's just what Lacy wants. Publicity for the money-making venture he's been planning. I'm glad I'm not tangled up with him anymore.*

She tapped her finger on the steering wheel and tuned the radio to a folk music station that was playing some of her John Prine favorites.

Later, when she was driving home on Friday, she had another thought about her situation at the firm. *The partners don't give a shit about morality or ethics. They only care about the huge fee income they get from Lacy and GENETECH.*

***

When the news about the Chinese babies reached Big Pearl, it revived talk about the issue involving Carson and Cesare Gastini.

The members of the school board had been watching Carson like a hawk for months. Several of them had wanted to fire him and be done with the issue.

Carson knew he was on thin ice. He took Cassie's advice to keep his mouth shut and Principal Joe Caldwell kept his word; he let Carson stay on as an English teacher so long as he did not talk about religion.

The Religion and Science Syndicate had also encouraged him to be careful. Jonas Markham had said, "Public opinion is against us right now. Let's wait for something to happen that will encourage people to take our side of the argument, or at least neutralize the strong secular sentiment that has infested our culture and the courts."

News about the Chinese babies was exactly what the Religion and Science Syndicate had been waiting for. The day after the story broke, Jonas Markham and Claire Evans called Carson back to their office for a meeting.

Claire said, "It's time, Carson. We want you to teach creation science one more time, and if you get into a scuffle with Cesare Gastini, then that is all the better."

***

A week later, on Tuesday, December 4, 2018, Carson strode into his English class to repeat the religious lesson that got him in trouble with the school board.

Once the students were in their seats, he began. But this time he started with the recent news from China.

"We heard last week that a Chinese scientist has used technology to make genetically edited babies, so-called 'designer babies.'"

The students squirmed, then sat perfectly still.

Carson stepped close to the first row. "This is what I was trying to warn you about earlier this year.

124

What Mr. Gastini has been teaching is not only wrong, it's dangerous. He thinks it is OK for man to fool around with God's creation, but that is pure nonsense.

"Seventy-three years ago, the eyes of the world focused on Big Pearl because a man called Bully Bigshot used his Eugenics Center to rid the world of people he didn't like. Hitler did the same thing in the Holocaust.

"I know I'll get in trouble for saying these things to you, but we must restore sanity to our schools. If Gastini can teach the religion of transhumanism, then I should be allowed to teach that God created man."

He then repeated all the points that had gotten him into trouble with the school board and dismissed class early.

That afternoon Carson was helping Slats prepare the team for an important basketball game when they heard loud chanting outside.

Slats told the boys to keep practicing, then said to Carson, "Sounds like they're pissed at you, Carson."

"Me or God?" Carson said. "I'll go outside and face them. Might as well get it over with."

Slats said, "I'll go with you; you might need some help."

"Thanks, but you better stay in here, Slats, or they'll fire you too."

Carson opened the door, and as soon as he stepped outside, Gastini and 15 members of TASAR pushed forward to confront him, chanting and waving an assortment of homemade signs.

Gastini got in his face and snarled. "You did it this time, Carson. You're gone, man. Gone, gone, gone."

Gastini laughed and stepped back, and as he did the TASAR group began their chant all over again. "Hey, hey. Ho, ho. God must go."

It was then that Carson saw several reporters and vans from the local TV stations.

He pointed at Gastini and spoke to the reporters in a loud voice. "Gastini teaches the religion of transhumanism in the classroom. He tells the kids that God did not create us. He teaches that the day will come when all beings will be created by technology and artificial intelligence."

Gastini shook his fist in Carson's face. "Carson Hamilton is a no-nothing. I teach science, not religion."

The TASAR chants started again, louder than before, and two members of the group waved their signs so close to Carson that he had to back up. He swung wildly and Gastini, pretending to be hit, fell to the ground writhing in agony.

It was all recorded, and the TV stations ran breathless accounts of the whole thing that night after promoting it throughout the day as "breaking news."

And it did not surprise Carson to see a high volume of social media traffic describing him in various ways. The worst called him "a religious fanatic determined to poison the minds of innocent schoolkids."

***

The next day, December 5, Monroe Slovak, the superintendent of the Big Pearl School District, suspended Carson. He delivered a written notice alleging that Carson's remarks to his English class constituted a material neglect of duty and good cause for termination.

The notice set December 19 for a hearing to be held at the Big Pearl High School.

Gastini and TASAR pushed the local prosecuting attorney to file charges for assault and battery, but he declined, saying there appeared to be no serious injury to Gastini and Carson's claim of self-defense was backed up by Coach Slats, who said he would testify that the skirmish was "a bunch of bullshit."

***

"Didn't I tell you to not do anything stupid?" Cassie said when Carson called to tell her what had happened.

"Yep, you did. But it's done." Carson said. "I plead guilty to being stupid, but the question is: Will you represent me before the board?"

"Yes, of course I will."

***

A few days later Cassie sent an email to the partners telling them that she planned to represent Carson before the school board on December 19.

Her phone rang a few moments after she sent the message.

It was Justin Bone, the managing partner. "I got your message. ... Come to my office. We need to talk."

Cassie dropped what she was doing and headed to his office.

As soon as she entered his office Justin Bone jumped to his feet and slammed his desk with an open hand. "Damn it, Cassie. We can't stop you from representing your teacher friend since you are doing it *pro bono*, but as of today you are no longer a senior counsel of this firm. You can stay on as an associate but …"

"This has more to do with Lacy and GENETECH than it does with Carson, doesn't it?"

"Believe what you will, but my decision is supported by all the partners. Your friend's trouble with the Big Pearl school board is going to create a lot of bad press. He'll be branded as a 'nut case' and so will you."

Cassie turned to leave.

But before she got to the door, Justin Bone gave an order. "One more thing: You need to move out of that nice office so that we can give it to someone more deserving."

Cassie stiffened. She started to give him the finger but decided against it.

***

Cassie was low sick on the drive home to Big Pearl that afternoon, but when she turned into the drive at Carson's house her spirits lifted. It had been like that since they were kids. Carson had a way of getting Cassie to look at the bright side of things.

He greeted her at the door with a big smile on his face.

"How do you do it?" she said.

"What?" Carson said, even though he knew what she wanted.

He put his arms around Cassie, and pulled her close, caressing a few strands of auburn hair that had fallen to her forehead.

She whimpered. "Your world is collapsing but you smile and comfort me."

"The good book teaches us to not worry about tomorrow." He kissed her on the forehead. "So, what's eating on you?"

Cassie hesitated, hugged him tight, then said. "Nothing that can't wait. Now let's get busy. The hearing is next week."

They listened to the recordings that Mona Sampson had made when he criticized Gastini's teaching about transhumanism.

Cassie made a few notes, and when the recording ended, she looked Carson in the eye. "You were clearly teaching religion in the classroom. You'll say you were responding to what Gastini was teaching, but the board is going to say that he was teaching science. What will you say to that?"

"I'll say the truth of it depends on how you look at it. If you believe in God, you will understand why I responded to Gastini. He thinks man is God. That's allows him to believe in transhumanism."

Cassie said, "That's an interesting argument, but the law says you cannot teach religion in public school. That's a truth we cannot deny."

Carson jumped to his feet and raised his voice. "Then the law needs to be changed so that we can counter Gastini's attempt to brainwash the students with his religious belief."

Cassie stared at him as he turned and looked out the window.

He's so sure about it ... gotta give him that ... and he may be onto something. I'm not there yet, but I need to keep an open mind if I'm going to help him ... I wish I could handle adversity the way he does ... what a way to live.

She got up and stood beside him at the window.

"Grace, Cassie." He said as he turned to face her.

"You asked how I do it; how I smile and don't worry. And that's the answer. My joy comes from the grace of a loving God."

He wiped a tear from her eye and kissed her, and they stood still for what seemed an eternity. Memories from long ago drifted by as they looked at each other, wondering why it had taken so long for them to get to this moment.

20

Trial

At mid-morning on December 19, hundreds gathered outside Big Pearl High School. It was cold and windy, but scores of people—some dressed up and some in overalls—stood in a queue that stretched from the front door of the school's Performing Arts Center to the street.

Some people waited in their cars and trucks, but others milled about waiting for the queue to start moving. A half-dozen reporters stood in a tight circle. They carried cameras and notebooks and seemed to be arguing about something.

Some people carried signs supporting Carson, but they were offset by an equal number of signs urging the school board to keep religion out of the classroom. The TASAR leaders wore their trademark outfits—all white from head to toe—but they had scores of supporters who were not in white. The RASS organization had a slight majority, and its supporters were easy to spot. They wore big red heart-shaped buttons with white lettering: Science + Religion.

An old man in one-gallus overalls stood on the steps leading into the building, shouting the same speech over and over: "In 1949 they tried young Kizzy for murder, but the trial weren't about her. It was about Bully Bigshot and what he was doin' at the Eugenics

Center. This ain't no different. Man is once again trying to take over God's job and us'n in Big Pearl know how to deal with such blasphemy."

A scrawny old man with a hunchback watched from afar. He stood on the bed of a pickup, tugging at the lapels of a soiled mackinaw, his eyes shaded beneath a broad-brimmed hat.

***

The Performing Arts Center quickly filled when the doors opened at 9:15 a.m.

The stage was set up like a courtroom; two counsel tables faced a long bench with chairs for the school board members. Cassie and Carson sat at the table on the left. Jeff Blaylock, the counsel for the school board, took the table on the right.

Cassie leaned toward Carson. "I can't believe that nitwit—Jeff Blaylock—is the school board lawyer. Remember him from high school days?"

Carson frowned. "He's a nice guy, Cassie."

Cassie said, "I'm sorry. I shouldn't have said that. It's funny, isn't it? The crazy stuff you remember about people."

Just before the school board members were to arrive, Cassie looked at the audience.

She saw Carson's parents sitting stone-faced next to a cluster of RASS supporters, and nodded to them.

They did not respond. She liked them and they liked her, but it was their nature to cast a buttoned-down image.

To her surprise, Kizzy was sitting on the second row next to Sheila Mason, one of the students in Carson's English class when he made his comments about Gastini.

Kizzy waved discreetly to Cassie when the school board members entered.

***

The members of the board took their seats and chairman Roscoe Morehouse gaveled the meeting to order.

"Today's hearing concerns Carson Hamilton and the comments he made about religion in his English class."

He read the charge, but it did not include the points Carson made the *second* time he spoke about Gastini to his English class.

Cassie got to her feet. "May it please the board: The charge you just read is incomplete. It summarizes the words that Carson spoke early this year, but it doesn't contain the important points he made the second time he spoke about Mr. Gastini's teaching."

The chairman said, "So, what's your point, Miss Davis?"

"It's simple. If you will amend your charge to accurately reflect what he said to his English class, we will admit that he spoke the words and that will save a lot of time."

Jeff Blaylock stood. "Do you have a record of what he said?"

"Mona Sampson, a student, recorded both sessions." Cassie handed a few sheets of paper to Blaylock. "I can call her as a witness, or I can introduce this word-for-word transcript of her recordings."

Blaylock looked over the transcript and nodded yes to the board.

Cassie handed transcripts to the board members, saying, "Please, notice that during the second meeting, Carson talked about the birth of genetically engineered twin babies in China, the world's first 'designer babies.' That is a volatile issue that has dramatically changed what many people believe about creation."

The chairman said, "OK, to save time, the board agrees to amend the charge to incorporate the transcripts."

Jeff Blaylock rose. "Since Mr. Hamilton admits the truth of the charge, I see no need to call witnesses." He turned to Cassie. "You can proceed, Miss Davis."

Cassie said, "Point of clarification, Mr. Chairman: Carson Hamilton admits to saying the words, but in no way does he admit that he has breached a duty or committed an ethics violation."

The chairman nodded.

Cassie said, "I call Cesare Gastini as our first witness.".

Gastini, wearing a too-tight olive-green suit with an oversized purple bowtie, took a seat in the witness chair.

Cassie began her questioning, and it was soon clear to everyone—especially Gastini, who squirmed and stuttered—that Cassie knew more about biology than the witness.

It was not long before she got Gastini to admit that he had taught about transhumanism on more than one occasion. She even got him to say that he had taught about it in connection with the Chinese babies.

But with each admission Gastini said, "But transhumanism is science; I only mentioned it because it something that is widely discussed in the scientific community. I was not proselytizing."

Cassie pounced, questioning his answer. "Oh, no?"

She stepped close and pointed at him. "Did you tell your students that you are a member of a worldwide organization called 'Humanity Plus?'"

"I don't remember whether I told them that or not. But so what if I did?"

Cassie said, "Didn't that organization used to call itself the World Transhumanism Association?"

"Yes."

"Then you surely believe, as a devoted transhumanist, that technology and artificial intelligence will lead us to an event you call the 'Singularity.' You believe, don't you, that we are coming to a point in human history when unstoppable scientific advances such as genetic engineering, technology and artificial intelligence will turn mortal humans into immortal gods. ... Isn't that so?"

The chairman whacked his gavel on the desk so hard that it broke.

"That's enough, Miss Davis. Mr. Gastini is not on trial. He has not been charged and will not be."

The crowd erupted. Their howling, jeering, and booing made a racket so loud that the chairman declared a 15-minute recess.

***

During the recess Cassie went to a quiet spot backstage to collect her thoughts. She sat down to study her notes, but she could not focus on the hearing. She thought of Carson, her mind drifting to other times and places.

I tried everything when we were kids to get him to have sex ... and he said no ... not before marriage. That's what he said. ... He still thinks that way because he is so certain that God has a plan for his life. ...

Now he's sitting here, on trial, the object of ridicule but he never wavers. ... I'm proud of him, and ... I've got to hang in and do my best. ... I wish I had his strength ... Hmmm ... What if he's right about all this ...

***

"Mr. Chairman, I call Carson Hamilton to testify."

Carson smiled at Cassie as he stood up and stepped to the witness chair.

Cassie got right to the point. "Carson, please tell the board in your own words why you said what you said to your English class."

"Gastini was feeding the students a line of baloney."

The audience howled with laughter and cheers of approval, but many people shook their heads in disapproval.

"Order!" The chairman pounded the table with his fist.

Carson said, "The students told me that Gastini's teaching went way beyond Darwin's theory. He was

138

telling them that man's inventions—artificial intelligence, technology, and genetic engineering—would take over the evolutionary process and that *homo sapiens* would be replaced by a new creation. In short, he is teaching that man is the creator of humanity."

Carson paused and rubbed his temple. "He is entitled to believe that, but it is not science—it is his religion—and it should not be taught in our schools.

"I got in trouble earlier this year when I told my class that I believed God created man, so I backed off.

"But when I learned about the 'designer babies' in China I decided I had to tell my students what is wrong with what Gastini believes."

Carson pointed to Gastini. "If he can teach his religion, then I should be able to teach mine. Furthermore, the U. S. Constitution presumes an omnipotent God, a creator. So why should we allow a phony religious belief to be taught under the guise of secularism?"

The audience began to rumble.

Carson stood up and shouted, "It's time for a level playing field. It's time for *total* truth, not the malarkey put out by the likes of Gastini."

Gastini stood up and shouted, "Hamilton is an idiot."

The white-garbed members of TASAR jumped to their feet, giving Gastini a raucous ovation.

The chairman struggled to get order, then said, "I think we have heard enough, Miss Davis. The courts have told us that religion cannot be taught in public school. Mr. Gastini says this transhumanist stuff is science and that he only mentioned it to the students because it is something that is widely discussed in the scientific community. He says he was not proselytizing.

"The board is ready to vote."

The crowd erupted. Some booed, some cheered.

Cassie said, "Well, Mr. Chairman, I would like to make a record of a few more points that can be raised when we appeal to the Circuit Court."

The chairman looked carefully at the audience. "Oh, all right, Miss Davis, but make it short."

***

Cassie stepped to the lectern. "Mr. Chairman and members of the board, it is fitting that this case is being heard in Big Pearl, Arkansas.

"In 1949 a man called Bully Bigshot lived here in Big Pearl. He practiced eugenics, the discredited belief that creation could be improved by sterilizing and aborting blacks, Jews, and the mentally infirm. He was convicted and sent to prison for his war against the weak. Hitler did even worse in the Holocaust.

"In 1968 the United States Supreme Court invalidated an Arkansas statute that prohibited the teaching of human evolution in the public schools. *Epperson v. Arkansas* was a landmark case decided after the Scopes Monkey Trial in Tennessee.

"In 1981, in the case of *McLean et al. vs. Arkansas*, the petitioners sought relief from an Arkansas law that said the teaching of evolutionary biology must be balanced with 'creation science.' The judge heard from several witnesses, then ruled that the law was unconstitutional. His decision was not appealed, but it was ratified in 1987 by a U.S. Supreme Court decision in a similar case from Louisiana, *Edwards v. Aguillard*.

"So, as you can see, Arkansas has been the epicenter of a long struggle over how to explain creation. Who's our creator? God or man?

"Carson Hamilton believes the reasoning that led the courts to decide as they did is flawed. It is outdated by recent developments.

"You can see from the exchange I had with Mr. Gastini that many people now believe in transhumanism, and they are hell-bent to make it the ultimate truth about creation. They do this with religious fervor; they make movies about it—*Transcendence* is one, *Galactica* is another—and they are filling the media with their arguments daily.

"Worst of all, they are itching to teach it to schoolchildren as if it is gospel truth.

"This is no joke. And the birth of designer babies in China is proof that we need to rethink the decisions that preclude the marriage of science with the religious explanations of creation.

"Mr. Gastini and his allies argue that their theories about the future of humanity is science, but it isn't. It is religion.

"The door should be re-opened by the Supreme Court to also allow teaching God's creation, the fundamental belief of all three major religions: Jewish, Christian, and Muslim.

"The so-called progressives say they want to separate science and religion, but the lines are now blurred. It is unfair to push traditional religion into a corner yet allow the teaching of transhumanism.

"Transhumanism is a religion. There may be no worship service, but they see evolution as a mystical force to be obeyed. In fact, some of them think Darwinian evolution just gets in the way of their quest to reach Utopia via science and technology. And, of course, to accomplish their goals there will be human self-sacrifice as we humans give way to what they call the 'Singularity.'"

"Can you imagine what those creations will look like? There'll be the outright mistakes, the so-called 'off-target edits,' but who knows what these creatures will think. And what will they believe? From whence will they get a sense of morality?"

Cassie stopped, took a sip of water, then summed up.

"Carson was right to say what he said to the students. We should link religion with science to find total truth. There are two ways to understand the relation of science and religious faith. The atheists use a warfare model. They reduce a complex equation to simple components, pitting one against the other.

"A better way—Carson's way—is to see science and religion as complementing each other to yield total truth and a richer and deeper vision of life.

"Consider this quote from a man named Sam Kean: 'The most profound change that genetics brings about might not be scientific at all. It might be mental and even spiritual enrichment: a more expansive sense of who we humans are, existentially, and where we came from, and how we fit with other life on earth."

Cassie folded her papers into a file and sat down.

The board members were stunned as the crowd began to clap, at first tentative. But when the applause reached a crescendo the cadre of uniformed TASAR advocates stood and turned their backs to Cassie and the board.

The board members shifted uneasily in their seats, looking at one another with odd, worried expressions.

The chairman said, "That's very interesting, Miss Davis, but the law is the law. ... It's time to vote."

The members voted unanimously to terminate Carson, but in a feeble effort to appease the Christian community the chairman and two other members whined about the spot they were in and suggested that Carson could continue to help Coach Slats if he did so on a volunteer basis and promised not to talk about religion to the student athletes.

The meeting adjourned. The TASAR and RASS activists split into clusters to pitch their respective beliefs to the media and anyone who would listen.

**

Later, Cassie told Carson, "You have the right to appeal to circuit court, but the result will probably be the same due to precedents."

Carson said, "I've made my point and I just want to get on with my life. The outside group, RASS, says the publicity and ongoing debate about the Chinese babies has set the stage for them to challenge the existing court decisions."

"Besides, I have an offer to teach at Saint James Prep. It's a fully endowed private school, so I will be able to teach Biblical creation if I want to."

Cassie laughed. "In English class?"

Carson said, "Why not, I've done it before." He thought for a second, then said. "I'll teach it in creative writing by saying that nothing is more creative than God's creation."

Carson laughed and poked her in the ribs. "How about that?"

PART VII--EPIPHANY

"I never made one of my discoveries through the process of rational thinking."

Albert Einstein

21

Wisdom

Cassie stood behind Kizzy brushing through long strands of gray hair as she hummed a slow version of "The Twelve Days of Christmas."

Kizzy looked at their images in the mirror. "People say we favor, even though my hair has gone from blazing red to dull gray to blazing white."

"You were a knockout when you were my age, Grandmother. They say that too."

"Don't start that 'grandmother' stuff. You've always called me Kizzy and I like that best."

Cassie smiled when she spied the determined look on her grandmother's face, and that triggered a fit of giggling that was soon joined by Kizzy.

When they composed themselves, Kizzy mumbled, "I can't believe I'm in my 90s." She sighed. "But I'm glad I was here to hear you and Carson lay it on 'em at the hearing. I almost shouted hallelujah when you said Big Pearl has been the epicenter of a great struggle."

Cassie said, "Strange, isn't it? That Arkansas and Big Pearl would be the place to settle such issues."

"Not really," said Kizzy. "The old battle with Bully Bigshot and his Eugenics Center was to stop a war against the weak. Bully was forcing sterilizations and abortions for people he didn't like: Blacks, Jews, the mentally infirm. He claimed he did it to improve the race."

Kizzy touched Cassie's hand. "Now you and Carson are trying to stop this Gastini guy and his kind. It's really the same fight. They think they can do a better job than God."

Cassie hugged her. "You said it much better than I did."

"Well, I lived through it, but a lot of good people didn't. This 'new eugenics' is no different from the 'old eugenics.' It's the poor, the weak—like the river rats of my childhood—who will be left behind. That's not good. It's what Bully and Hitler wanted to do."

***

At 10:25 a.m., Carson knocked once, then opened the door and shouted, "Are you all ready to go? We need to be on time because it's Christmas Day."

Soon thereafter the three of them eased into the pew that Kizzy and Stefan commandeered as their own the first Sunday after they married.

The opening hymn was Mendelssohn's "Hear My Prayer" and when the choir sang Stefan's favorite verse— "O for the wings of a dove" —Kizzy touched Carson with one hand and Cassie with the other.

The preacher's message built on a single theme: "Jesus was born among us to make real the vision of creation for all humanity and all God's creatures. The relationships between God and humanity must be set right."

When the service ended Cassie pulled a necklace from her blouse to show Carson the golden pendant that Kizzy had given to her when she was a young girl. She traced the Hebrew letters on the pendant with her finger.

Kizzy beamed. "Stefan gave that to me when I was a girl. It's Hebrew lettering, Carson. It spells Chai! It shows respect for 'Life and the Living God.' It helps us to understand that life goes on."

Cassie said, "When Kizzy gave it to me, she said, 'Now you're safe. Enjoy every day of your life.'"

Carson said, "Perfect."

After church, they went to lunch at Sweetcheeks' Café. Then Carson drove them home.

When they were alone Kizzy said, "Don't let Carson get away, Cassie."

22

The Thinking Spot

Cassie slept late on Wednesday, the day after Christmas. When she got up Kizzy was in the kitchen sipping a cup of coffee, reading the newspaper. "Hey, sleepy-head."

"Hummmmm." Cassie rubbed her eyes and plopped down next to Kizzy.

"I thought you'd be going back to Memphis today."

"I thought about it—I've been off for two weeks—but that can wait. I'll go back next week, after New Year's Day."

"Good plan," Kizzy winked. "That'll give you more time with Carson."

"Yep, there's that. But I also need time to think about *everything*: The stuff we talked about, what the preacher said, and what I'm going to do with the rest of my life."

"Those are big questions," Kizzy wrinkled her brow. "When I was young, I used to go to my thinking spot to work out such things."

"I've never had a thinking spot." Cassie looked away. "Maybe that's my problem. Too much doing and not enough thinking."

Kizzy giggled, then began to draw a map on a piece of scrap paper. "Everybody needs a thinking spot, Cassie."

She pushed the map across the table.

"Go to my spot. It's a pretty day and the old stump is still there. I made some big decisions there and have never regretted it."

***

The land behind what used to be Bully Bigshot's cotton gin was a mix of wetlands with patches of higher ground thickly covered with a stand of native hardwoods. Cassie followed the map over a scrubby trail to a clearing marked with an X.

She saw a huge stump in the clearing, exactly where Kizzy had scribbled the word "stump" on the map. *This is it... Kizzy's thinking spot... the last place where she saw her grandpa alive.*

Cassie sat down on the stump. Her first thoughts were about Kizzy's life when she was a river rat. *No running water ... no electricity ... kinfolks that could barely read ... they believed in the law of the river ... there was good in that ... nature and doing what's natural ... but now she's a Christian ... and so is Carson.*

Cassie stayed for a while thinking about her heritage, but soon she began to shiver. *There's more to*

151

think about, but it's cold. Besides, this is Kizzy's spot. I need my own spot, and I know just where to go.

***

Cassie settled into a cubicle near the front windows of the Big Pearl Library and Veterans Center. *This is where Kizzy met Olivia, the woman who encouraged her to read Jane Austen. ... I've been coming here for as long as I can remember, but I always came to read. Today I'm here to think.*

Three hours later, Cassie put away the books she had taken from the shelves. *I need to find Carson ...my sounding board ... there's a lot that I need to tell him.*

***

As soon as Carson opened his door Cassie rushed in, embracing him as never before. She kissed him twice, then twice more, sobbing all the while. Then she took his head in both hands and looked into his eyes. "I'm such a fool, Carson. But I'm coming to my senses after all these years."

He kissed her and when their lips parted, she said, "I love you."

"I've waited years to hear you say those words in that way." He kissed her again. "I've always loved you; you know that."

Cassie kissed him again, then cast a solemn look. "I've been thinking a lot lately. Today I went to Kizzy's

152

©

old thinking spot and then I went to my own thinking spot, trying to make sense of everything."

She pulled him to a corner table. "Will you sit here with me and just listen? There's a lot I need to say."

Carson nodded and swept a finger across his lips to show that they were sealed. Then he leaned back in his chair.

Cassie took a deep breath. "I respect your commitment to abstinence, but I have not followed your lead on that." She paused, looking for the slightest sign of disapproval, but his expression did not change.

"There were a few times in high school and when I first got to Memphis, but they didn't mean anything. And, I dated a client, Lacy Franklin, the CEO of GENETECH. He's the man I was with the day you saw us at Paulette's Restaurant on Mud Island. And …"

Carson held up his hand. "I know you want me to just listen, but all that is ancient history as far as I'm concerned. … If you are done with Lacy there's no need to say more about any of that."

Cassie broke down crying, then hugged him. "You're so good, Carson."

He said, "I can tell there's more you want to say, but let's adjourn to Sweetcheeks' Café for a bit of dinner."

"Good, because I *do* have more to say, and it concerns what I argued at the school board hearing."

***

The waitress at Sweetcheeks' seated them in a quiet corner. The café was not crowded, so she told them to take their time.

Cassie took a sip of iced tea and settled back in her chair.

"The preacher got my attention yesterday when he said, 'The relationship between God and humanity must be set right.'

"But Gastini and the transhumanists don't see it that way.

"They see man as a god who will use technology, genetic engineering, and artificial intelligence to transform the humans of today into entirely new beings.

"They say it's inevitable because the birth of 'designer babies' in China has opened a door that cannot be closed."

Cassie slammed the table with her palm. "I disagree."

Carson grinned big. "I like the sound of this."

"It's as you said: It all comes down to one's view of the world. Those with a God-centered view will say no to designer babies. Those with a man-centered view—like the transhumanists—will rationalize and say it's OK.

"I ran across a book at the library that puts it in perspective. In *The Case Against Perfection* the author, Michael Sandel, says man thinks he can and should control everything."

Carson tapped his finger on the table. "That's always the problem. Hubris. The fatal flaw."

Cassie nodded. "Sandel says man's 'drive to mastery' threatens to alter the nature and meaning of parent-child relationships."

"How so?" Carson said.

"People who are driven to design and manufacture their children will not appreciate the gifted character of human powers and achievements.

"The point is: We should love our children for who they are, not for what they are."

"That's what God wants," Carson said.

Cassie said, "It comes back to what the preacher said: 'The relationship between God and humanity must be set right.'"

Carson said, "God has to be in the picture. That's what Gastini and his kind refuse to accept."

Cassie said, "To be honest, I was on the wrong side of this for too long. I think I've always had a touch of the 'drive to mastery' myself. It's OK to a point—I excelled in school and I'm a damn good lawyer—but in the end a worldview that puts God in the center is the only way to find total truth."

"Amen." Carson smiled. "Preach it, Cassie."

She laughed. "I don't mean to be preachy, but I'm a little bit like a reformed drunk. There's a lot on my mind that I need to get out, especially the thoughts I had when I went to Kizzy's thinking spot."

Carson said, "Take your time."

"Kizzy was raised on a ramshackle houseboat down on the Black River. They were called river rats. She lost her grandparents and her mother and had to live with a no-good man she called her 'make-do stepfather.'

"They lived by what they called 'the law of the river.' It was a hard life, but Kizzy survived by reading and learning a better way to live.

"Then she married Stefan and became a Christian.

"Kizzy says Jesus is the best way to understand nature and the good things she learned while living by the law of the river.

"That's what the preacher meant when he said the 'relationship between God and humanity must be set right.'"

Cassie took Carson's hands in hers. "It's taken me a while, Carson. But I understand now why you were willing to risk your career. Gastini and his kind are teaching that humans will evolve into a perfect creation. That creation will be an entirely new being made by man, not God."

23

Deciding

Cassie took a deep breath as she pressed the elevator button that would take her to the offices of Barton, Bone, and Dempsey.

It was Wednesday, January 2, 2019. Three weeks had passed since she had left for Big Pearl to represent Carson before the school board.

When the elevator doors opened the receptionists greeted Cassie and pointed to a big conference room where a meeting was in process.

The senior partners and three associates were laughing and yukking it up with several people she did not recognize. Just then, a man in a blue suit turned just enough for her to recognize his profile. *Lacy! Damn ... he's the last person I wanted to see.*

Justin Bone waved for her to come into the conference room.

What the hell is this?

She avoided eye contact with Lacy when she entered the room, speaking first to the partners, then the associates. Bone introduced her to the men she did not know, and when she turned to face Lacy the room got very quiet.

Lacy said, "GENETECH needs you, Cassie. We're entering a new and complicated era of genetic engineering now that the Chinese babies have opened the door."

Cassie, dumbstruck, looked to the managing partner.

Justin Bone smiled. "Lacy has told us all about his plans for GENETECH and we want you to pick up where you left off. ... As senior counsel, of course."

Lacy said, "Come on back, Cassie. Help us get ready for what is sure to come, a huge demand for designer babies. ... We're not going to do anything in the U.S. until it's legal, but things will change. ... It'll be just like *in vitro* fertilization. That started offshore, but now it's normalized; it's legal and everyone is doing it."

Justin Bone interrupted. "How about it, Cassie?"

Cassie glared at Lacy, then faced the partners who were sitting together.

She shook her head, squinched her lips and bellowed, "No way."

She turned to leave without saying more, but after taking a step she whirled around to enjoy the stunned looks.

"It's wrong! ... I come from a place where this kind of thinking got out of hand. I'm talking about the old eugenics craze that brought death and misery to so many people.

"What you all want to do will lead to a new eugenics, and I want no part of it."

Justin Bone stood up. "Now calm down, Cassie. Lacy and GENETECH have a good reputation and so does this firm. Take some time to think about it. This will be a good thing for the firm, and for you personally. ... Why don't you ..."

"I don't need any more time to think." Cassie made a fist but kept it at her side. "I quit!"

"Hold on, Cassie." The oldest partner, Sam Barton, stood up next to Justin Bone and shook his finger at her. "You have every right to leave, but I must warn you: You can't take private client information with you."

Cassie stiffened. "I know about the privilege and will abide by it—legally—but I cannot unlearn what I know about this issue, and about people like Lacy.

"And as for this firm: You all are letting greed and insensitivity distort your thinking. That is what caused the tragedy in Big Pearl back during World War II days.

"If you represent Lacy knowing what you know, you are just as guilty as he is. Indifference to evil is a kind of dry rot that will destroy you in the end."

Cassie threw her keycard to the office on the table.

"I'll be out of here within the hour."

She stared at Lacy and wheeled to leave, and when she got to the door she turned around and blew them all a sarcastic kiss.

PART VIII—RESTARTING

"You can't go back and change the beginning, but you can start where you are and change the ending."

C. S. Lewis

24

Together

Carson opened the front door of the small office building kitty-corner from the Big Pearl Library and Veterans Center.

"I got it," Carson shouted. "A half-gallon of off-white, and a package of rollers."

Cassie, in coveralls speckled with paint, used the back of her hand to push a lock of hair from her forehead.

Carson set the can of paint on the floor and pointed to a 3 x 5 hand-painted sign on the front window; black Baskerville lettering trimmed in gold.

"Smitty did a good job." Carson said as he put his arm around her and read the sign. "Cassie Davis, Attorney at Law."

"I never thought I'd open a law office in Big Pearl," Cassie chuckled. "But a couple of clients in Memphis are sticking with me, so it's going to work out fine. Now let's get busy and finish. I want to open for business by the first of March."

Carson grinned. "You a lawyer, and me a schoolteacher. Both of us right here in Big Pearl. That's just as it should be."

***

St. James Prep—a well-endowed parochial school—was quick to hire Carson after the Big Pearl school board fired him.

The small but powerful members of the Big Pearl school board joined with the TASAR leaders to spread malicious gossip about Carson to justify his firing. They called him an "evangelical loony" and encouraged people to shun him, but their slurs did not work.

The firing made Carson a spectacle of sorts, but a majority of people in Big Pearl admired him for trying to stop Gastini from teaching what they called "weird stuff."

Civic clubs for miles around invited him to speak, as did other social and educational organizations.

He politely declined every invitation.

Cassie knew why he did not want to speak out. He had revealed his reasons to her the day they finished painting her law office.

"It's just not my cup of tea, Cassie. I don't like all the attention. I'll take my turn teaching Sunday School once a month, but I don't like publicity. All I ever wanted in life was to teach English, coach sports, and get into school administration when I get older."

Cassie said, "That's *all* you ever wanted?"

He pulled her close and kissed her. "You, of course. I've always wanted you. You know that."

As they embraced, Carson felt the warmth of her breasts and for the first time he let his hardness lay against her so that she could feel it.

They stood still, enjoying the magical moment. But Cassie pushed away. "Abstinence, Carson. Abstinence."

She kissed him. "You've saved yourself for 30 years. Let's wait and do it your way."

Carson nodded yes. "So, does that mean you will marry me, Cassie?"

"Yes, silly. I've wondered if you were ever going to ask."

They kissed again and held each other tighter than before.

The feverish spell was slow to cool, but when it did, Carson said. "Let's announce our engagement on Easter Sunday, and then I want you to be a June bride. … I want everything to be done exactly right. I've waited so long for this."

***

The sanctuary of the First United Methodist Church of Big Pearl hummed with excitement as the congregants settled into pews. The chancel rail was lined with fresh lilies, an Easter tradition that lifted spirits and filled the church with the sweet scent of resurrection.

Kizzy sat between Carson and Cassie admiring the lilies she sponsored in memory of Stefan; Olivia, who encouraged her to read; MeeMaw and Grandpa, who taught her to love nature and the law of the river, and Birdie, the river rat who won the Medal of Honor and came home to save her from Bully Bigshot.

The choir processed through the nave, singing one of Stefan's favorites, Mendelssohn's Easter hymn "The Strife is O'er." The acolytes and pastor followed the choir down the aisle, and once they were in place the service began with a prayer. Then the pastor asked Carson and Cassie to come forward.

The congregation rustled, whispering busy talk as Carson and Cassie walked, hand in hand, to the chancel rail. But when they turned to face the congregation the sounds of excitement gave way to total silence.

Carson put his arm around Cassie, smiled and took a deep breath.

"You all know us. We've been a twosome since we were 10 years old."

There was a moment of silent anticipation before he continued.

"And today, I'm proud to announce that we are engaged to be married on June 15."

Carson kissed Cassie, and they hurried back to Kizzy's pew to boisterous applause and scores of congratulatory comments.

Carson's parents, in the pew behind Kizzy, smiled and gave high-fives to those sitting nearby.

Reverend David Orloff let the racket subside, then said, "I look forward to conducting that wedding." He then used the joy of their engagement as a beautiful segue to the glory of Easter and the resurrection of Jesus.

Kizzy cried throughout the service, but her tears were tears of joy. She touched the mother's ring on Cassie's finger. "I wish Charlene could be here, but she's looking down."

When the service ended dozens of well-wishers crowded around them as they were leaving the church, but a hunchbacked old man stood off to the side, watching their every move. And when he left the church, he put on his broad-brimmed hat and made a beeline for his truck.

***

Cassie's solo law practice in Big Pearl started well. Two laboratories in Memphis put her on retainer the day she opened. And she landed two local cases that would surely end with litigation, giving her a chance to show homefolks the trial skills she had learned in the big city.

Carson was happy as a clam, teaching English and coaching. Once a month, he taught Sunday School for a class of teenagers, and warned them about the dangers of science run amok.

He continued to get invitations to speak but encouraged Cassie to accept them in his stead.

The local newspaper, the *Big Pearl Free Current*, asked Cassie to write an op-ed about why she decided to come home to Big Pearl after her successful start in Memphis. She took the occasion to remind folks that she was the granddaughter of Kizzy, a river rat who brought down the evil Bully Bigshot and his Eugenics Center.

The piece made two other points: First, it told that she got interested in genetics when she learned that her mother was dying of breast cancer due to the BRCA gene, and second, it warned readers about the transhumanists, saying their plan to redesign humans was being driven by computer engineers and biohackers with no concern for ethics or morality.

The article drew a huge number of letters addressed to the editor. Most were supportive, but some said her views were old-fashioned. One of the negative letters got Carson's attention as they were having breakfast the day it was published.

He slammed the newspaper down on the table and pointed to the letter. "This stupid letter must have come from Gastini or one of his acolytes. It says you and I are standing in the way of something that is inevitable."

Cassie frowned. "Let me see."

She took the newspaper, read the letter, then put the paper down. "You know, Carson, the more I study and think about all this, the more I agree with you. These people must be stopped. It's one thing to improve humans, we're all for that. But the fanatical drive to mastery, the urge to genetically re-engineer God's creation has got to be stopped."

"Amen," Carson said.

Cassie grimaced. "The transhumanists are so into nanotechnology and artificial intelligence that they see our biology as an obstacle, a limiting factor to their ultimate goal: Singularity."

"Never fear, Cassie. God will give us the ammunition we need."

25.

Wedding

June 15, 2019 was a hot, muggy summer day, typical for Arkansas.

At 10:30 a.m., the First United Methodist Church of Big Pearl was filling up, but people were still coming in. Outside, latecomers were driving around looking for a place to park.

The engagement of Carson and Cassie had been the talk of the town since it was announced on Easter Sunday, and this was their wedding day, a special occasion for Big Pearl.

Cassie waited in the pastor's office with Kizzy. They were standing in front of a full-length mirror primping, making last-minute adjustments to the lace-trimmed wedding dress.

"Can you believe it, Kizzy? Seems like just yesterday that Carson and I first met. We were 10, and now we're 30 years old."

Kizzy looked at their images in the mirror. "That ain't old, dearie." She pointed to her own face. "This is old."

They laughed and hugged, but soon they heard the organ playing, and a few minutes later everyone was in place at the altar and the preacher was asking the familiar questions.

And when they kissed as man and wife, the crowd roared its approval.

Carson looked into Cassie's eyes just before they turned to go back up the aisle and caught his breath. *Her eyes—those tender hazel eyes—have the sparkle and freshness they've always had. Yes. Like always. But I see more. Odd now to see something new. But there it is. ... Love, yes. But trust and sharing and the soul. I see all that and I know she feels the same.*

Cassie felt the difference too. As they left she looked at the stained-glass window over the door to the narthex, glowing from the light outside, *That's our story, Carson.* The rainbow of many colors—arched from one side of the window to the other over a chalice and loaves—told the story of God's love. *Carson, after all these years, we are together.*

Later at the reception they did all the customary things. They visited with every well-wisher who wanted their attention, and when that was done Cassie tossed her bouquet to a cluster of young girls. As luck would have it, Mona Sampson, the girl who taped the speech that got Carson fired, caught it.

Then, as they were about to leave the church, an old man approached Kizzy who was standing next to Cassie. He said, "My uncle was Sully Biggers, you knew him as Bully Bigshot. ... I've waited too long to tell you how sorry I am for all the misery he caused you and the folks who lived down on the river. ... He was no good and got what he deserved."

Kizzy hugged the man; he cried but so did she. They consoled him but soon he was gone, as quietly as he had come.

"There's a lot of good in the world," Kizzy said. "Now you all get going. It's time to start your honeymoon."

***

They spent their first night as man and wife in Memphis at the Hilton. Carson had shown some interest in staying at the Pyramid, but Cassie said she did not like the place.

They arrived late, famished. They sent their bags to the room and went directly to a nearby restaurant. Carson was eager to eat and go to bed, but Cassie talked endlessly about the wedding, recounting conversations she had with scores of people at the reception. Carson listened, but mainly fiddled with his food and watched her every move. *She's beautiful, and now—finally—she's all mine. ... my wife ... how will it go ... my first time ... I was right to wait ... I think ...*

Cassie broke his reverie. "Hello. Where are you?"

"I'm ready to make love to you, that's where I am." He laughed. "In fact, that's what I've been ready to do since we were 10 years old."

***

They made love all night and again in the morning, but at 8:30 they packed up, checked out, and made the short trip to the Memphis airport.

They spent their second night at the Hilton in Providence, Rhode Island. Their lovemaking was just as urgent as it was on the first night, but Carson was a quick learner and by morning they knew for certain that their life together would be as good as either of them had ever imagined.

They took a limousine for the one-hour and 15-minute trip from Providence to Hyannis, Massachusetts where they boarded the ferry for Nantucket Island.

As the ferry pulled away from the dock, Carson smiled big. "This is perfect. Happily married to my childhood sweetheart and heading to Nantucket, the place where Ishmael shipped out with Captain Ahab aboard the whaler *Pequod*."

Cassie poked him. "So, you're a romantic as well as a good lover."

"Just good?" Carson poked her back.

"OK, you're a terrific lover! Now, tell me again about your fascination with *Moby Dick*."

"I've taught it, of course, but I love the story and I've always wanted to come here." He pointed in the direction of Nantucket. "In Herman Melville's story

Captain Ahab is a man obsessed, so much so that the world has no existence apart from him and his all-sufficient self.

"The critics say that Melville's writing is antithetical to the writing of Ralph Waldo Emerson, the leading transcendentalist of that era who preached self-reliance. Now, I love Thoreau, Walden Pond, and all that, but Melville showed through Ahab what happens when you think the world revolves around you."

Cassie said, "I get it. You're equating Captain Ahab with Cesare Gastini."

"In a way," said Carson. "Today's transhumanists *are* obsessed." He sneered. "But Gastini himself is a wimp."

Cassie got tickled when she saw the look on Carson's face.

And when he saw that she was laughing, he laughed too. And soon the two of them were deep into another full-scale laughing fit.

Carson said, "Well, that's enough about Gastini. Let's enjoy this magnificent place." He pointed to the island which had come into view. "There, on the east end; that's where our cottage is. Ten days in Heaven."

26

Challenge

Cassie stood in front of her law office to watch the sign painter put the finishing touches on the gold-trimmed black letters. "You do good work, Smitty. I like the sound of it: Cassie Davis Hamilton, Attorney at Law."

"So do I, ma'am. Everybody likes Mr. Carson."

Smitty left, but Cassie stayed there for a second. *Yes, he is a good man. ... took me too long to see that ... those other guys ... especially Lacy ... not going to dwell on that ... ever again.*

***

Cassie spent a couple of days catching up on paperwork that had accumulated during their honeymoon.

But on Wednesday, July 3 she left the office early so that she and Carson could drive to Little Rock and get there before rush-hour traffic.

They took a room at the Doubletree overlooking the Arkansas River and the sights in North Little Rock. Once unpacked, they left the hotel to stroll along the interesting trails and bridges that allow walkers to enjoy both sides of the river.

Carson pointed to the ballpark as they walked by Dickey-Stephens Field, the home of the Arkansas Travelers. "We've got great seats for tomorrow's game against the Springfield Cardinals."

Cassie nodded. "I know you love the game, but I'm looking forward to seeing all the kids and the Fourth of July festivities."

They walked across the bridge leading to the Clinton Presidential Center and meandered their way a few blocks beyond the Old State House Museum and the Doubletree to have dinner at Doe's Eat Place.

"This is going to be a great weekend, Cassie. Let's have fun and not talk about the Gastini mess."

***

The next morning at breakfast Carson turned to the sports section of the *Arkansas Democrat-Gazette* to check the baseball scores. "The Travs lost last night to the Naturals, 5-7."

Cassie opened her iPad, scrolling through headlines. Suddenly she stopped scrolling and read a headline aloud: "Third gene-edited baby born in China."

Carson said, "I thought we were taking a break from all that."

"This is big, Carson. Listen."

She skimmed through the story, reading excerpts. "It's from the Massachusetts Institute of Technology—*MIT Technology Review*—so that's a credible source.

"It says Stanford bioethicist William Hurlbut told *Agence France-Presse* that he'd talked extensively to He Jiankui—the disgraced Chinese scientist—about a third gene-edited baby. ... He expected it to be born in June or July of this year.

"So, they're not for sure, but experts believe the baby may already have been born."

***

As soon as they got back to Big Pearl, Carson called Jonas Markham of the Religion and Science Syndicate.

"I emailed you a story this morning that Cassie saw in the news July 4. It was about a third designer baby born in China."

"I got it and forwarded it to Claire Evans."

Carson said, "We have a few ideas that may be helpful."

***

The RASS leaders came to Cassie's law office the next day.

After greeting one another, Cassie said, "In my opinion the report about the birth of a third genetically edited baby rejuvenates the argument we started with the school board."

"We agree," said Jonas Markham. "We made some calls as soon as we heard the news and several other groups are ready to move out."

Carson said, "We're just getting settled so you all will have to take the lead, but we'll do what we can."

"We're grateful for any help you can give," Claire said.

Cassie said, "Here's the bottom line: We've entered a new era that may cause the Supreme Court to take a fresh look at its Establishment Clause rulings."

Jonas gave her a quizzical look.

Cassie opened her iPad. "Here's what I mean: In a 1981 Arkansas case, Federal Judge Bill Overton distinguished creation from evolution in his decision to strike down a state law that required the teaching of creation science. He said: 'Although the subject of origins of life is within the province of biology, the scientific community does not consider origins of life a part of evolutionary theory. The theory of evolution assumes the existence of life and is directed to an explanation of how life evolved. Evolution does not presuppose the absence of a creator or God.'"

She let that sink in, then said, "Pope Francis recently made a similar observation. He said, 'The evolution of nature does not contrast with the notion of creation, as evolution presupposes the creation of beings that evolve.'"

Claire said, "What's the significance of that for us?"

Cassie closed her iPad. "This new era has a growing number of transhumanists like Gastini. They see 'Darwin's biological evolution' as an obstacle to the glorious new 'creation' that will come from man's ingenuity, *i.e.,* nanotechnology, artificial intelligence, and genetic engineering."

Carson scoffed. "Who needs God in a world like Gastini's?"

Cassie said, "That's the point. The transhumanists are not concerned with original creation *or* Darwinian evolution. They believe an entirely new being will be created by man."

Jonas rubbed his forehead. "The new era is not here yet, thank God."

"Not entirely, but it's coming," Cassie frowned. "Several colleges offer workshops focused on transhumanism, which they define as 'the belief that the human race can evolve beyond its current limitations through the use of science and technology.'

"In the workshops students are urged to combine their scientific and technical know-how with artistic and aesthetic concepts to make prototype devices showing

179

how man will bridge the gap between human and technology."

Claire gasped. "If the transhumanists can teach young people that man is the ultimate creator, is that not a religious belief? ... I mean ... such a belief displaces God as creator *and* Darwin's theory of evolution."

Cassie said, "In the Arkansas case, Judge Overton said there is no way teachers can teach the Genesis account of creation in a secular manner.

"But he ruled that they could teach evolution."

She opened her iPad again. "This is from his opinion: 'Evolution is the cornerstone of modern biology, and many courses in public schools contain subject matter relating to such varied topics as the age of the earth, geology, and relationships among living things. Any student who is deprived of instruction as to the prevailing scientific thought on these topics will be denied a significant part of science education.'"

Jonas said, "How could a court allow the transhumanists to teach their account of creation? Virtually all religions say that God is the creator and that creation is divine. Teaching that man—not God—is the creator is wrong."

Carson said, "That's the issue in a nutshell."

Cassie stood up. "It's a framework for going forward. If you stop Gastini and his kind from preaching the transhumanist version of creation it will lead to a big fuss over what teachers can and cannot say in the classroom. That's because they believe, and are determined to teach, that man has a better idea than God."

Carson said, "Amen! Gastini and his kind cannot resist the urge to claim that their beliefs will lead to Utopia."

Cassie looked at Jonas and Claire. "So, that's where you should focus your legal effort. Don't relitigate the creation science issue. That's an uphill climb. Start with what we've talked about today and see where it leads."

***

That night after dinner, Carson and Cassie walked to the L.W. "Birdie" Barden Memorial Park on the town side of the Black River, a splendid setting high above Curly's Fish Market, a Big Pearl fixture since World War II days.

They sat down on a cedar park bench and watched the boats go up and downriver.

Cassie said, "I'm glad RASS and some other groups are going to take the lead on the legal front. TASAR and the Gastini crowd are way too angry. They'd tar and feather you if given the slightest chance."

"I'm not worried about that," Carson said. "But I do wonder: Do you think Jonas and Claire will stay on it?"

"I hope so."

Carson said, "You told them to start with what you advised them to do, and then you said, 'Let's see where it leads.' What did you mean by that?"

Cassie frowned. "I think transhumanism is so entangled with the sciences of technology, genetic engineering, and artificial intelligence that teachers will be compelled to discuss it as they teach about evolution.

"Gastini, for one, will force the issue. He says evolutionary biology gets in the way. For him and others like him it as an impediment."

Carson grunted. "Transhumanism—if not rebutted—will become the default explanation of creation. That's not fair, and it's not right."

"Precisely." Cassie took his hand, and they headed home.

PART IX— PERSEVERE

"The true soldier fights not because he hates what is in front of him, but because he loves what is behind him."

G.K. Chesterton

27

Wounds

On Monday afternoon, July 8, nine member organizations of RASS issued a joint news release stating that they were planning to take legal action to ban the teaching of the transhumanist theory of creation in public schools on the grounds that it is a religious belief that violates the Establishment Clause of the First Amendment.

The release triggered several comments—pro and con—on radio and television talk shows that afternoon and evening. And the Tuesday, July 9, edition of the *Big Pearl Free Current* carried a front-page story about the release quoting Jonas Markham who said his group was raising an entirely new issue and that the syndicate "did not intend to relitigate the issue of creation science."

The paper also quoted Claire Evans, who thanked "Carson Hamilton for his help in advancing this important cause."

***

On Wednesday morning, Carson received a phone call from a gravel-voiced man who said he saw the story in the newspaper and claimed to have some important information about Gastini that might help the cause. The man said he would give him what he had if Carson would meet him alone at 2 p.m. that day at Ray's Bait Shop just north of Big Pearl.

The man said, "I'll be drivin' my ol' Ford pickup—it's a black 'un."

Carson asked him his name and the man said, "It's Jude, but I caint get involved, so let's keep this 'tween me and you."

***

Carson arrived a few minutes after 2. He saw two sedans, but only one truck parked in front of Ray's. It was an old black Ford, but no one was in sight.

Carson parked and started toward the front door of Ray's. He had taken only two steps when the bullet struck, and he heard the gunshot. It like someone had stuck a red-hot poker in his side. He tried to walk, but stumbled, and fell forward just as a second shot rang out, hitting high up on his left arm.

The shooter hurried by Carson, cackling and spewing hatred as he got into this truck. "Ha! …Nothin' like takin' out a Holy Joe."

Carson turned on his side just enough to see that the man was hunchbacked.

The storekeeper and two customers ran outside just as the black Ford turned out of sight. Ray pulled off his T-shirt and pressed it against Carson's belly to stop the bleeding. One of the customers said, "I'm calling 911 for an ambulance and the cops."

Ray inspected the wounds and said, "I got gut-shot in Vietnam, Carson. And you'll be fine so long as it didn't hit something vital."

A customer said, "Who was it, Carson?"

"He was hunchbacked, that's all I know."

Ray said, "That's Judas. He's a sorry SOB. Crazy as a road lizard."

Carson moaned, but nodded. And as he drifted into the early stage of shock, the ambulance came.

***

Dr. Miles Kimbrough, a 2006 graduate of Big Pearl High School, was tending patients in the emergency room when the ambulance arrived with Carson.

Cassie arrived a few minutes later, but by then Carson was in the operating room. She tried to pump the nurses for information, but it was a half-hour before she got the good news.

"He's a lucky man, Cassie," said Dr. Kimbrough. "The abdominal wound is clean with no serious damage to the small intestine. The gunshot to the upper arm was just a flesh wound. So, the bottom line is: He's in great physical shape so he should heal up rather quickly. I'd say six weeks or less."

"Thank God," Cassie said. "And thank you, Miles."

He nodded. "Have you heard anything about the man who shot him?"

Cassie said, "He's dead. The police cornered him at his place which is a couple of miles from where he shot Carson."

"So they shot him?"

"No, he shot himself. The police don't know much right now but they are checking the records to learn more about him." She brushed a lock of hair from her forehead. "Can I see him now?"

"Absolutely. He's been asking for you."

***

"You're a lucky man, Carson." Cassie leaned over to give him a kiss on his forehead. "The doctor says you are going to be OK."

"Blessed, Cassie, blessed. God looks after us fools, you know."

"What were you doing at Ray's? You never cared much about fishing."

'The guy called me and said he had some information about Gastini and would only give it to me. So, I went to meet him and he shot me. That's all I know." He took a sip of water. "He told me his name was Jude but I hear it was Judas Marchant. That fits him better, don't you think?" Carson giggled, but winced as he did.

Cassie frowned. "You can't laugh, and besides, it's not funny." She squeezed his hand. "He's dead, you know. Shot himself. The police are looking into it."

Carson squeezed her hand. "This is the first time I've been in a hospital. I want to get out of here, but Miles says I need to stay here tonight for observation, but he thinks I'll be able to go home tomorrow or the next day."

"He's a smart man, Carson. Do what he says."

***

On Monday, July 22, 12 days after the shooting, Carson was home with Cassie. An Arkansas State Police investigator came by and summarized what they had learned about Judas Marchant.

"He was a first-class whacko." Sergeant James Gadson opened his notebook to tell about the places Marchant had lived before moving to Arkansas. Then he said, "He bought 10 acres just outside Big Pearl just 15 months ago; the double-wide trailer was part of the deal. We found a huge number of magazines, tabloids, and scandal sheets put out by extremist outfits, cults that rail against religion. Some were pornographic, but the constant theme was atheism."

"So, he tried to kill Carson because he is a Christian?"

"That's the theory that fits best," Gadson said.

Cassie said, "Was he a lone wolf?"

"Yes. So, we are planning to close the case."

***

A week later, on July 29, Richard Rankin, the FDA investigator assigned to the U.S. House Committee to investigate genetic engineering abuses, came to see Cassie at her office in Big Pearl.

"We believe the man who shot Carson was acting on his own. He was an atheist who hated Carson for speaking out about Christianity. It appears that he was provoked by media coverage of the Big Pearl High School issue about what can and cannot be taught in public schools."

"We learned that from the local police," Cassie said. "So, that's not why you are here. Right?"

"Correct. I'm here to talk about the issue we talked about some time ago. Now that you are not with Barton, Bone, and Dempsey, I … "

Cassie interrupted. "I'm still bound by the attorney-client privilege."

"I know, but the privilege doesn't keep me from telling you what we are up to. And I think I owe you that."

Cassie leaned back in her chair. "So?"

"Our investigation took off after the first Chinese babies were born, and after the third baby was born it intensified. We now believe that Lacy Franklin is running a rather complicated enterprise that involves money laundering, bribery, and contributions—some legal, some not—to political and government officials.

"The purpose is to make money, by hook or crook, from the business of designing babies for wealthy people. Their plan is to start offshore where it may be legal, even as they are bribing key people to soften U.S. laws and regulations that might get in their way."

Cassie nodded.

"Our inquiry, as you can see, has widened, and if the House Committee elects to make a criminal referral to the Justice Department the case will be investigated by the FBI and others."

He paused, but Cassie said nothing.

Rankin said, "I saw where the RASS organization may go back to court over the dispute that Carson had with Gastini. I don't know that our inquiry is related to that in any way, but it's another reason I wanted to bring you up to speed. I mean … you never know."

Cassie said, "Thanks for coming by. I appreciate the heads-up about your investigation. But, for your information, neither Carson nor I will have an active role in any legal action that RASS may take."

28

Choosing

On Tuesday, August 27, the first day of the fall term, Carson walked down the hallway of St. James Prep and stopped at the door outside his classroom. It was time to start his second-period senior English class, but the hallway was oddly quiet, and the door to his classroom was closed.

He looked around, then opened the door. And as soon as he stepped into the room his students stood up and cheered, shouting an assortment of welcomes.

Carson smiled, said thanks, and motioned for his students to sit down.

"Thank you for that nice welcome, but as you can see, I am fully recovered and that means I will be as tough as ever if you butcher the English language."

The students laughed, and with that Carson began his second year at St. James Prep. Later that day, he met the new head coach, Mickey Fowler, who warmly welcomed him to be his assistant coach.

***

Meanwhile, Cassie was busy with her new life as a solo practitioner of the law in Big Pearl. It was quite a change from practicing with Barton, Bone, and Dempsey, the largest firm in Memphis. Her new colleagues—small-town lawyers in and around Big

Pearl—derisively referred to all big city lawyers as "tall building lawyers." But they respected Cassie's intellect and warmed up to her after Carson was shot.

One lawyer, 95-year-old Harvey Douglas, took a special interest in Cassie. He had long since quit taking cases that required a lot of paperwork, but he could still shuffle into the courtroom to defend an accused, and when he did the young lawyers would gather to hear him make his closing argument. Harvey's mesmerizing technique improved as he aged. And that is what made him a living legend.

The day after Carson got shot, Harvey came to see Cassie at her office. He hobbled in, unannounced, and painfully lowered himself into the Queen Anne chair fronting her desk. He was wearing his trademark suit, a double-breasted getup that might have fit when he bought it in 1980. Now it hung loosely on his gaunt frame.

He grunted, then leaned back to relax. "Whew. Gettin' old ain't for sissies." He laughed aloud and touched his handkerchief to eyes that had the fiery look of a man in his prime. It was a captivating look that spoke volumes.

Cassie smiled. "Hey, Mr. Douglas. What can I do for you?"

"I don't need a thing, Cassie. I'm just here to say how sorry I am that Carson got shot. You kids didn't deserve that, but it's the sort of thing will make you stronger if you'll let it."

Cassie could see that he wanted to say more, so she smiled and nodded. "Thanks, Mr. Douglas."

"Your grandmother Kizzy went through a rough patch when she was a young girl living on the river. I remember it like it was yesterday. She stood up to Bully Bigshot and single-handedly put a stop to the evil he was doing at the Eugenics Center. I was just 20 years old, but what she did is what made me want to be a lawyer."

Cassie said, "All that was before my time, but I know the story. It influenced me too."

He smiled and gave her a thumbs-up. "You and Carson just need to stay strong. This town has a streak of hate lying just beneath the surface. It's been there since the days of Bully Bigshot, but you can't let that get you down. Just keep fighting for what you believe is right. That's what I learned from your grandmother and it's a rule to live by."

Cassie started to speak, but the old man was struggling to get to his feet, so she went around her desk to help him.

"That's all I came to say, Cassie." He thanked her with eyes that suddenly seemed tired. "Stay strong like Kizzy."

***

Throughout September and October Cassie busied herself at the law office. She took in enough fees to cover the rent and pay a secretarial assistant. And she landed a wrongful death case—thanks to a referral from Harvey Douglas—that was sure to yield a substantial fee.

Carson, meanwhile, had settled in at St. James Prep. He especially liked coaching the football team even though they were not having much success on the field.

Then, on Halloween, while having an early dinner with Kizzy at Sweetcheeks' Café, the news came that Harvey Douglas was dead. He had collapsed that afternoon when he stood to deliver his closing argument to a jury sitting in judgment of a young boy accused of stealing a second-hand car.

Harvey left specific instructions that he wanted a simple graveside service with no eulogies, except for one by Kizzy.

Scores of people, some in their finest but most wearing work clothes, crowded around Harvey's gravesite. Fittingly, it was in the pauper section where lay Kizzy's family, Birdie, Olivia, Shirley, and dozens of nameless river rats.

When the preacher yielded to Kizzy she spoke softly. "I first met Harvey Douglas when he was a boy. He was a lifelong friend and I will miss him, but so will hundreds of poor people who turned to Harvey for advice when the law was after them for one reason or another.

"He didn't aim to get rich, but he leaves a rich legacy. That's because he devoted his life to helping poor folks—especially young people—find their way. He was a fighter, a fair and gentle fighter. If I could think of something that fit him better, I would say it, but I can't. So, goodbye, Harvey. You fought the good fight. May you rest in peace."

***

In the weeks before Thanksgiving, Cassie wrestled with whether to tell Carson about what the FDA investigator had told her about Lacy and the congressional investigation into his plan to get rich by creating designer babies.

She decided against it, but the more she thought about all she knew, the angrier she got.

A fanatical man, driven by the hateful activities of TASAR and Carson's effort to stop the transhumanists, had shot her husband and then killed himself. The RASS group was working around the clock to build a new legal action to deal with Gastini and his kind.

In the face of all that, Cassie had gone back to her law practice, letting others do the fighting.

She kept thinking of the words that Kizzy spoke at Harvey Douglas' funeral: "He was a fighter, a fair and gentle fighter."

Cassie's anger at herself soon turned to guilt, then shame when she realized she had chosen the cowardly route of indifference.

***

On Sunday morning, November 2, she went to church with Carson and Kizzy, but she tuned the preacher out.

I'm a mess ... all stirred up inside. ... I should do more ... What's my life been about? ... BRCA gene yes. ... killed Mother ... studied microbiology ... then the law ... then—ugghh—got too close to Lacy and his wrongheaded scheme to make designer babies ... then Carson ... always Carson ... and now ... he got shot but he's a fighter ... things have come full circle ... Now ... back in Big Pearl ... what's for me? ... Harvey was a gentle fighter ... Me?

As they left the sanctuary Kizzy said, "That was a good sermon."

Carson agreed, then whispered to Cassie who had ignored Kizzy's comment. "You seem to be out of it this morning. Are you OK?"

"I'm fine. Let's take Kizzy to lunch at Sweetcheeks' Café. Then let's go back to the park. Just the two of us. It's a nice day, and once we are there, I'll tell you what's on my mind."

***

Cassie pointed to the ripples on the river as they walked toward their favorite cedar bench in the park.

"It's a little breezy and chilly, but I wanted to come here because this is where we came after our meeting with Jonas and Claire the day we talked about the best way for them to handle the Gastini problem."

"Is this about them?"

"Not directly. They and the RASS group are ready, willing, and able to take whatever legal action is necessary to battle transhumanism.

"But the issues I'm worried about are greater than Gastini and what can be taught in the schools."

Carson blinked, then gave her a puzzled look. "Greater? What could be greater than taking that creep down?" He poked her in the ribs. "C'mon, Cassie. Level with me. What's this about?"

She frowned. "Don't laugh, Carson. This is serious, and I've been doing a lot of thinking about it.

"Gastini *is* important, but genetic engineering, technology, and artificial intelligence are moving at warp speed while the decision makers—judges and politicians—diddle, ponder, and obfuscate. Their top speed is slower than molasses."

Cassie stiffened and lowered her voice.

"I've been speaking and writing about the dangers of genetic engineering for some time. In my book I called for a moratorium on germline gene editing. You know, heritable genes, designer babies, things like that."

She shook her head. "But now I'm beginning to think that the line barring germline editing may not hold."

"Why?"

Cassie bellowed, "Because the powers-to-be are in the process of caving in."

She paused, shook her head, and unleashed a rapid-fire explanation.

"In the beginning the scientific community agreed, universally, that the line should not be crossed. The American Medical Association put out a strong statement saying that germline manipulation could result in unpredictable and irreversible results.

"Others weighed in, worried that such modifications might be used for enhancement purposes—like designer babies—rather than for curing or treating disease or restoring lost functions.

"And everyone—everyone—agreed that such enhancements would be so expensive that only the wealthy could afford it."

"But now ..." Cassie groaned and flicked her hand as if shaking off a noxious bug.

"The big shots are beginning to say that the clinical use of germline editing should be 'revisited' on a regular basis. They're saying 'scientific knowledge is advancing, and societal views are evolving.'

"That's the mushy language of compromise. They're getting ready to move the line that they said should not be crossed. And I know for a fact that some people are working hard to make it happen."

Carson said, "So, what is all this leading up to? What does it mean for you? For us?"

Cassie stood up and made a fist. "This is being driven by rich people who are spending a fortune to lobby Congress for the right to bust the germline." She stamped her foot. "We need to fight this."

"OK, count me in." Carson said.

"I've been thinking of something really wild, something that could change our life. But if it doesn't pan out I can always go on with my law practice."

"Stop the suspense, Cassie." Carson giggled, and so did she.

When they composed themselves, Cassie looked him in the eye.

"I'm going to run for Congress."

"What?" Carson gasped.

29

Politics

At noon on November 11, 2019, the last day to file, Cassie, Carson and Kizzy drove to Little Rock, leading a caravan of avid supporters: Mona Sampson, Sheila Mason, and scores of Carson's former and current students; Jonas Markham, Claire Evans and several members of RASS; Coach Slats Monroe, Coach Mickey Fowler, and a dozen longtime friends from church, St. James Prep, and Big Pearl High School.

Cassie handed her paperwork—a political practices pledge, affidavit of eligibility, signature collection affidavit, and the notice of her candidacy for the office of United States Representative—to the filing official.

Then she stepped to an area reserved for media interviews. A gaggle of reporters and cameramen gathered amidst the supporters.

"I am Cassie Davis Hamilton of Big Pearl and I have just filed the paperwork required to become an Independent candidate for Congress."

Her entourage cheered, and as they quieted down an old reporter said, "Can you get the 2,000 signatures you'll need to qualify?"

"Easily." Cassie pointed to her supporters. "These good people have assured me that they will have more signatures than that in the first week."

That set the crowd off again and Mona Sampson shouted, "Amen, we could get 10,000 if we had to."

Carson nodded to two boys from St. James Prep who quickly positioned two easels next to Cassie. One was a huge blowup of a front-page news story from the March 6, 1945 edition of the *Big Pearl Free Current*. It displayed a photograph of a man in handcuffs and leg irons. The other was a 3x5 foot picture of the old Big Pearl Eugenics Center.

Cassie pointed to the easels. "This sordid bit of history tells a lot about why I am running." She pointed to Kizzy. "My grandmother—I'm so proud of her—lived through it, the victim of discrimination and hard times.

"The news story tells about Bully Bigshot, an evil man who ran a despicable outfit called the Eugenics Center. He wanted to rid the world of people he despised through abortion and 'better breeding.'

"My grandmother had a lot to do with sending Bully Bigshot to prison, where he died. She taught me the dark side of genetics.

"Then, when I was 10 my mother died of breast cancer; she had the dreaded BRCA gene.

"That's why I have made it my life's work to study biology, genetics, and the law. I want to make sure that science is used for good, not evil.

"These are the reasons why I am running for Congress.

"Our government must deal with the potential benefits and risks associated with the use of CRSPR 9 gene editing, including the ethical, social, and legal implications of CRSPR-related biotechnology products.

"It is urgent. But the politicians and judges are not keeping up. They do not understand, or they cave in to special interests who will bribe them if necessary to get their way.

"I know these issues inside out and backwards. I have written a book on the subject and have brought several copies for you to peruse.

"The legal struggles about evolution, like the one that involved my husband at Big Pearl High School, will continue, but I can do more with my education and legal expertise as a member of Congress.

"When I told my grandmother Kizzy that I intended to run for Congress she said, 'Go for it! What's happening now is no different from the old eugenics. It's just a new kind of eugenics.'

"She's right. The eugenics wars are back, in a new, more virulent form. We must get this right or it will lead to another war on the weak. One based not on race, but on financial ability."

Cassie stepped back from the microphone, but the old reporter asked a question she was ready for. "Why are you running as an Independent?"

She smiled. "Easy. What I have outlined here today is the most important issue our country and the world must decide. It has nothing to do with political preferences. I'm not going to Congress to help the Republicans or the Democrats. I'm going there to do what is right. I will work for the people and do what is best for the country."

30

Ugliness

On the day after Cassie filed to run for Congress, Carson scoured the newspapers and checked every radio and television station to assess the coverage. He read every word of a long story in the statewide paper but was happiest with the coverage she got in *The Big Pearl Current*.

He pointed to the color photograph and banner headline. "Front page! It's a great picture of you and you can see the old stories about the Eugenics Center in the background."

Cassie snickered. "Wait 'til some reporter skins me alive. Then we'll see how much you like politics."

Carson said, "Old Slats keeps up with politics. He says there's no such thing as a bad story if you are running for office. He says it's all about name recognition."

"Ha! I don't agree with that, but we'll find out soon enough."

***

Cassie had it right; their euphoria was short-lived.

On Thursday, three days after Cassie's announcement, the first negative ad appeared on television.

Kizzy saw it and called Cassie. "I just saw an ad, and it's terrible. ... There's a video of you and Carson at the school board hearing ... they're saying he's a religious nutcase ... and you are against the separation of church and state. ... It's awful, Cassie."

Cassie said, "I know. We saw it."

"Who's doing this?" Kizzy said.

"Some outfit I never heard of, but I bet TASAR is behind it."

***

The ad ran for 10 days, a heavy buy that inspired several news stories about Carson's trouble with the school board. Cassie's message about the evils of genetic engineering gave way to stories about the separation of church and state.

Cassie and Carson spent most of their time on defense assuaging supporters and contributors who feared the ads were causing irreparable damage.

The negative television ads were followed by a 10-day run of radio and newspaper ads, all with the same scurrilous message.

Cassie learned that the television and radio ads were paid for by a group called Protect the Kids.

***

On the last day of the radio ad campaign Richard Rankin paid another visit to Big Pearl. He found Cassie in her law office, doing paperwork.

"How's your campaign going, Cassie?"

"Well, contributions have dried up, and my supporters are dispirited." She shook her head. "Other than that …"

Cassie laughed at herself. "Politics ain't beanbag, is it?"

Rankin said, "Cassie, Protect the Kids is just a front group. The money is coming from Lacy Franklin, but he is laundering it through TASAR and others.

"I'm not surprised." Cassie said.

Rankin said, "There's nothing I can do about it right now. I just wanted you to know what my confidential source is telling me."

"Thanks, Richard."

"And, for what it's worth, we know that you are just one target. They are going after everyone who is speaking out against transhumanism. This is not about church and state, although that's the nature of their attack on you. Most transhumanists are atheists. They'll go after anyone who's in their way, and that includes God."

Cassie pointed to a copy of her book that was on her desk. "That's a good point, Richard. I touched on it in my book, but I like the way you said it better."

31

Disease

For the next seven weeks Cassie worked nonstop to keep up with her law practice and still have time to meet prospective voters. She showed up at public events, especially well-attended ones, and never missed an opportunity to speak and shake hands with voters.

She did her best to fend off bad press, but the reporters would have none of it. They relentlessly portrayed her as a lawyer who tried to tear down the delicate balance between church and state.

And to make matters worse, the negative ads reappeared for an extended run, this time alternating pulses of television with radio.

The TASAR demonstrators stalked Cassie, recording her speeches, and making videos of her supporters. They posed as defenders of the Constitution, schoolchildren, and the 'American way.' And they never mentioned Gastini or transhumanism.

***

On New Year's Day 2020, Cassie was downhearted, so Kizzy arranged for her to say a few words to a gathering of veterans at the Big Pearl Library and Veterans Center. Kizzy went with her and urged her to say something nice about an old friend in her speech.

When it came time for her to speak, Cassie followed Kizzy's advice. "I wish Uncle Mac could be here. He meant so much to my grandmother in the old days. I could sure use some of his homespun wisdom now that I'm running for Congress."

The crowd of veterans cheered, especially the old vets who knew Uncle Mac. One of them hollered out, "He was the smartest man in the county, Cassie, but you'll do to tie to. If Kizzy's for you, Uncle Mac would be too, and that's good enough for us."

The vets cheered, and the old man who spoke started handing out Cassie's campaign literature, saying, "Get everyone to vote for Cassie's. She's a fighter."

***

Cassie, rejuvenated, campaigned hard for the remainder of January, and on February 1, 2020, Mona Sampson called a meeting of the supporters who had agreed to circulate the petitions that would qualify Cassie as an Independent candidate for Congress.

Thirty people showed up, and 10 days later they had collected 2,323 signatures, easily exceeding the minimum requirement of 2,000 signatures.

Cassie Davis Hamilton, an Independent candidate, was officially in the race for Congress.

"There's no backing out now." Carson said.

"Who said anything about backing out?" Cassie punched the air with her fist. "Let's get going!"

***

Cassie picked up the pace. She spent the next two weeks traveling to every corner of the district, redoubling her effort to offset the damage done by the onslaught of negative ads.

But no matter how hard she worked, the talking heads on TV and the political cartoonists were dead set against her campaign. They pointed to opinion polls showing her with less than 10 percent even though the negative ads had increased her name recognition. The prevailing explanation for her poor standing was that she was too closely identified with fanatics determined to preach religion in the public schools.

Cassie worked harder. "It's looking bad, Carson, but we've got to keep fighting and get this thing turned around."

***

On Tuesday, February 11, 2020, the *Big Pearl Free Current* carried a story on page 5 about a strange new virus. The story reported that an American citizen had died of the virus a few days earlier in Wuhan, China.

Cassie and the other candidates for office carried on even though news reports about the virus intensified as the disease spread throughout South Korea, Iran, and Italy.

On February 29 there was news of a death in Washington state, the first on American soil. That spurred more talk about the virus. People were concerned, but they soldiered on.

***

On March 3, Arkansas politicians held watch parties to celebrate or bemoan the outcome of elections held that day. Cassie paid some attention to the returns, but as an Independent candidate her name was not on the ballot that day.

Cassie and Carson spent the evening with Kizzy, eating pizza and watching the returns.

One newscaster mentioned Cassie's poor standing in the polls, opining that she was no threat to either of the major party candidates.

"Baloney!" Kizzy wadded up her napkin and threw it at the TV.

"You can't pay attention to the polls," Kizzy said. "I know from experience that public opinion can change overnight.

"I got thrown in jail and had to stand trial for killing Cormac, a no-good if there ever was one.

"But Birdie came to my rescue. In the midst of my trial, he proved what Bully Bigshot and his cohorts were doing to poor people at the Eugenics Center.

"And when that got out, I got off on a hung jury, but Bully Bigshot went to prison.

"From that day to this the people of Big Pearl have put me on a pedestal.

'So, the point of my story is: Keep fighting, don't ever give up."

***

Cassie and Carson worked harder than ever after that.

The negative ads stopped, but TASAR opened a local office in Big Pearl. They said it was to work against RASS, but the people who worked there openly campaigned against Cassie.

Even so, hundreds of people signed up to help Cassie, and by the second week of March things were looking up. The Cassie for Congress campaign had turned a corner.

On March 11, Cassie and Carson sponsored a party at their home to watch the Arkansas Razorbacks beat the Vanderbilt Commodores 86-73 in the first round of the Southeastern Conference Championship game. Like most Arkansans, they were hoping the Hogs would get an invitation to the NCAA tournament, March Madness.

The victory over Vanderbilt was sweet, but it turned out to be the last game of the season because earlier that day the World Health Organization had declared a pandemic. And President Trump, having already banned travel to the U.S. from China, issued an order banning travel to the U.S. from 26 European countries.

Life in America changed dramatically two days later on March 13, when the president declared a national emergency. People were instructed to stay home, wash their hands, and maintain social distancing; some began wearing masks.

Cassie canceled all campaign events and urged her supporters to listen to the experts.

By the end of March most of America was in lockdown, with the New York City metropolitan area as the epicenter. Businesses big and small were forced to close; people were marooned at home, some officially quarantined. Millions upon millions lost their jobs, a nightmarish development for a nation that had just posted record high economic numbers.

Surreal images filled social media, the newspapers and television. Famous sites—Times Square, Champs Elysée, Trafalgar Square—were empty. No people, no cars, no buses. Thousands of airplanes were parked, idled in a paralyzed world, waiting hopelessly for passengers who were now too scared to travel. Scene after scene of empty streets, empty ballparks, empty everything except for the essential workers who were wearing masks and staying six feet distant from other mask-wearing citizens.

People were dying. The whole world was in shutdown.

Cassie's campaign for Congress came to a screeching halt.

***

Shortly after the shutdown began, Cassie made the mistake of asking Kizzy for the second time if she would like to move to Revelation Senior Living.

Kizzy exploded. "I told you before, Stefan and I built this house and this is where I'm going to take my last breath, not in some damn warehouse for the old and decrepit."

That was that. Carson and Cassie moved in with Kizzy, who complained of a sore throat the very first night they were there.

"Let's call Doctor Baldridge. They're saying you should get tested if you have symptoms."

"I'm fine, and I'm not going to the doctor. I was raised tough, on the river, and don't you forget it." Kizzy took a swig of Listerine, gargled and spit into the sink.

"I'll be alright tomorrow."

And she was.

***

Cassie and Carson did their best to carry on a virtual campaign for Congress.

They posted photos, videos and factual snippets on Facebook, Twitter, and Instagram. But the few responses they got showed high interest in the pandemic and little interest in Cassie's campaign for Congress.

Carson tried to pacify Cassie, to no avail.

"Let's face it, Carson. COVID 19 is killing my campaign. There's no way we can get our message out now."

PART X—REVIVAL

"When you dig a well, there is no sign of water until you reach it, only rocks and dirt to move out of the way. When you have removed enough, the pure water will flow, said Buddha."

Deepak Chopra

32

Hope

On Palm Sunday, April 5, 2020, Cassie, Carson and Kizzy were lazing around the house, listening to the local radio station, KBIG, when they heard the sweet voice of Dolly Parton talking about covid-19.

"Listen." Cassie said.

Dolly answered the interviewer, "I think God is in this … He's trying to hold us up to the light so we can see ourselves and see each other through the eyes of love. … I hope we learn that lesson. I think when this passes, we're going to all be better people."

Cassie sat bolt upright. She said, "We can see ourselves!"

Kizzy and Carson stared at her.

Cassie slapped her leg and whooped. "That's it. … This pandemic mess is giving us a chance to 'see ourselves.'

"And that gives me a fresh way to explain why I am running for Congress."

Cassie noticed their confusion, so she slowed down to make her point.

"Look, in recent years we've adapted to a deluge of technology: iPhones, social media, instant news, and scientific discoveries too numerous to count.

"We've also grown comfortable with innovative medical procedures, transplanted organs, amazing new prosthetic devices, and scads of other treatments that were unthinkable just a few years ago."

She paused. "But now we find ourselves in a strange new world."

Carson said, "The world of social distancing?"

"Yes." Cassie pondered for a second. "We need to do what we're doing to bend the curve of sickness. I get that. But social distancing *is* forcing us to live in a strange new way.

"It separates us, cordons us off, keeps us away from loved ones, even the dead and dying."

She got up, walked to the window, and looked out.

"We're getting a glimpse of what it would be like to live in an even stranger world, the crazy world of the transhumanists who aim to achieve immortality by merging man and machine. Theirs would be a tightly controlled world filled with automatons—robots, androids, and cyborgs—and designer babies made for the rich and genetically engineered to lord it over the rest of humanity."

Carson scoffed. "Gastini's world."

Kizzy broke her silence. "This social distancing they're making us do is 180 degrees from the way we lived when I was growing up. We lived by the law of the river, close together, and we took care of each other in the hardest of times. Now we can't go to church or ball games, and worst of all we can't look in on neighbors. Being separated breeds selfishness, and that is no way to live. The Indians who lived on the river near us called selfishness *wetiko*. It's a condition that makes humanity its own worst enemy."

"Amen to that, Kizzy," Carson said. "I don't like it either. Forcing us to separate may help us beat the covid-19 virus, but it feeds the virus of selfishness."

Kizzy said, "Good point, Carson." She began to sing softly, in the crackling voice of the elderly. "People who need people are the luckiest people in the world." She giggled. "I stole that from Barbra Streisand."

Carson applauded. "Right on, Kizzy."

Cassie sat down by Kizzy. "Forced separation is contrary to man's nature, and it's a hard thing for freedom-loving Americans to swallow. But it does give us a chance to show what life would be like in the strange world envisioned by Gastini and the transhumanists."

Kizzy said, "Gastini and his kind are just modern-day versions of Bully Bigshot. It's eugenics by another name."

"Well, that's why I'm running for Congress. We need to stop them before it's too late."

Carson said, "We need to get that message out. Let's start tomorrow with a video on Facebook, Twitter and Instagram."

***

On Monday morning, Cassie starting writing scripts for videos incorporating some of the thoughts they had talked about over the weekend. Meanwhile, Carson converted the living room into a makeshift studio complete with lighting, sound, and a videocam mounted on a tripod.

Cassie's first script tied her concerns about genetic engineering of the germline to social distancing. She meant for it to grab attention to set the stage for later videos and media posts, all with the hope of cutting through the incessant drumbeat of news about covid-19.

Cassie read the first draft to Carson and Kizzy.

Kizzy was polite, but she did not like the script.

Cassie said, "What's wrong, Kizzy?"

"It's terrible. Too lawyerlike. Too technical."

Carson laughed, but Cassie stiffened. "Well, germline editing is a complicated subject."

Kizzy said, "I know it is but bear with me. ... I remember a story my grandpa used to tell about General Ulysses S. Grant. He had a rule that none of his orders could be sent to his officers unless they were first read to the dumbest man in his army. If he understood it, then the order was sent to the officers. Grant said he did it that way so that no officer could claim later on that he didn't understand the order."

She laughed at her own story, then gave Cassie a hug. "So tone it down, Cassie, and write it so that everyone can understand it."

Cassie rewrote the script several times before Kizzy gave her approval, and at 4 p.m. they were ready to shoot the video.

Carson operated the camera. Kizzy critiqued.

The first three takes ended in disaster. Cassie got frustrated and went outside to be alone.

In a few minutes she returned. "OK, I'm ready. This is going to be a good one."

Carson turned on the lights and then signaled for her to start.

Cassie took a deep breath and looked squarely into the camera.

"Hi, I'm Cassie, and if you like social distancing, you're gonna love what's in store for you if we don't do something to stop it.

"Curious? I'm talking about the crazy idea that man can design babies better than God.

"You heard me right. Billions of people believe that. It's called transhumanism. Remember that word—transhumanism.

"If we allow those people to mess with our genetic code to design babies there's a lot that can go wrong, and we'll be stuck with the mistakes they make. That's because changes to the germline will pass down to future generations.

"I don't like the strange new world we are in, and I sure don't want to live in the strange world envisioned by the transhumanists.

"I'm Cassie Davis Hamilton, and I'm running for Congress to stop the madness. Don't mess with our germline. Leave it like God made it.

"Please join our cause. Go to CassieForCongress.com and follow this hashtag: #GermlineNoNo."

She smiled into the camera and Carson looked at the clock. "Sixty seconds exactly. Perfect!"

They posted it on Facebook, Twitter, and Instagram, then, after dinner, streamed *The Candidate* with Robert Redford from Amazon Prime.

Kizzy nodded off early in the movie and went to bed before it was half-over.

Cassie and Carson watched it to the end.

***

On Tuesday morning after breakfast, Cassie looked at Carson. "I'm almost afraid to see how the video was received."

Carson said, "No time like the present." He opened his iPhone and checked the apps. "Good grief, Cassie, your post has gone viral.".

Kizzy said, "See? They got it when you simplified it. Now you know for sure that folks hate social distancing and they don't want designer babies or any of the other stuff that Gastini is pushing."

Carson giggled. "We're also getting a lot of activity on your website." He cheered. "And donations. We're getting donations too."

33

Winning

By Thursday, a trend developed. There was a handful of negatives claiming that the video politicized a health issue, but most responses were encouraging. All but a few agreed with the idea that social distancing gives people a glimpse of what life would be like in a strange new world.

One post, however, hit a nerve. The writer accused Cassie of over-simplifying a complex issue.

Cassie read the post aloud to Kizzy and Carson.

"This one stings a little, but it's the price I have to pay for converting a complicated issue to simple language." She looked at Kizzy. "General Grant probably got the same criticism from a few of his officers."

Kizzy chuckled. "Probably. But remember: He did win the war!"

Cassie said, "Good point. But ours is another kind of war. It is a battle royal of ideas. TASAR wants the fight to be about teaching Christianity in school. But we have shifted the fight to new ground, a field of battle that reaches far beyond the classroom.

"Our enemy is transhumanism, an evil philosophy that means to replace humanity as we know it.

Carson applauded. "Well said, Cassie. And that's a fight we can win."

"*Must* win, Carson," Cassie said.

***

On Good Friday, the *Memphis Star-Ledger* carried a small piece on page 4A about a congressional inquiry of GENETECH and its CEO, Lacy Franklin. The article, based on a tip from an unnamed source, suggested a range of genetic engineering activity that might run afoul of existing standards. For most readers, the article was hopelessly vague. But Cassie could read between the lines thanks to the updates she had received from the FDA man Richard Rankin.

Cassie cheered.

Carson said, "What's to cheer?"

"There's a lot I'm not allowed to say about my work at the Memphis firm, but here's something I can say: The genetic engineering issue—designer babies and all that—is not going away.

"We're on a hot trail, Carson, so let's double down.

"Let's make another video about how social distancing is giving us a peek of what it would be like to live in a strange new world. But this time let's get rough. Let's be specific. Let's tell how editing the germline could result in tragic mistakes that would be heritable. You know: Pass down from generation to generation."

Carson said, "Let's put in that weird idea they have about uploading our memories to the Internet so we could live forever."

Cassie grinned. 'That's a stretch, but some who call themselves transhumanists have said things like that."

They made a second video—tougher than the first—and posted it on Good Friday. Cassie ended the video saying, "I'm Cassie Davis Hamilton, and I'm running for Congress to stop the madness. Please join our cause."

***

On Saturday before Easter Sunday, Cassie did a telephone interview with the local radio station and made the point people were shifting to technology such as Zoom, WhatsApp, and other gadgetry to stay connected.

The host, Charlie Gray, said on the air that he had changed his opinion about Cassie's campaign. "To be honest, I didn't think you had a chance, but my listeners really like what you've been saying on social media."

Cassie said, "This new connectivity is a poor substitute for the close and natural connections that we love and trust—connections that have worked for us throughout history."

The host said, "Well, you are making the most of it. I saw a news story just this morning that an Arizona congresswoman likes what you've been saying. She said she is going to put in a bill to stop most germline editing."

"That's good to hear. We are making progress," Cassie said.

"Yes, but can you win? After all, no one can campaign right now due to the shutdown."

Cassie said, "We can't campaign in a traditional way, that's true. But neither can the opposition.

"But we have hit a nerve with our social media postings. So that is how we will campaign—a virtual campaign—and that is how we will win. Check out the polls. They are trending in our favor and the money is flowing in. TASAR's effort to kill our campaign with negative publicity has failed."

Charlie Gray ended the segment with a question. "So, you don't think the transhumanists can take us to Utopia?"

Cassie said, "The Utopia that the transhumanists covet is folly. They are driven by hubris and self-interest. That's not Utopia. It's Y—O—U—topia."

34

Resurrection

Easter Sunday was a beautiful day. The forecasters had predicted scattered thunderstorms and showers, but that was of little concern to most Arkansans. They were staying home, sheltering in place to comply with government orders to maintain social distancing.

Kizzy said, "Empty churches on Easter Sunday. What's the world coming to?"

Carson said, "We could watch one of the megachurch preachers on TV, but Pastor Orloff is live-streaming the Easter service from First Methodist.

Let's do that." Kizzy said. "I'd rather hear Brother David."

Cassie said, "This is the first Easter since I've gotten serious about my faith and wouldn't you know it, the church building is off limits."

***

At 10:55 a.m. Carson streamed the service on his iPad.

Carson pointed to the screen. "Look at that, would you. Brother David is there, all alone."

Kizzy said, "Just watch, he'll make the most of it."

And he did, standing at the chancel rail instead of the pulpit.

"This empty sanctuary is a shock, but it reminds us of the first Easter when the women went to the tomb and it was empty. Jesus had risen, as promised.

"The empty tomb proclaims that life does not stop when death comes. There is more to life than physical existence, more to existence than self.

"That is our belief, but will this break with tradition weaken our spirit and drive us apart? Or will this moment of forced separation, rouse a fresh hunger for congregating and connecting?

"The question comes as the world faces a host of new and puzzling challenges, but this empty church—like the empty tomb—proves that the life of the church does not end, just as the empty tomb proclaims that life does not stop when death comes. God lives, Jesus lives, and the Holy Spirit lives. The door has not closed. It is open. These pews may be empty, but the spirit is here, and it goes with you wherever you may be. Just look around. You'll see it in the selfless acts of those who are caring for the sick and elderly, the first responders, and the hard workers who keep the shelves full at the grocery.

"Through plagues and wars, upheavals and revolution, the faith has endured. Now we must answer the call once again. Let's face it with a new and rejuvenated spirit. After all, we have a great victorious savior who went through worse and came out on the other side.

"If we meet the challenge, I'm sure Jesus would say, 'We'll done, good and faithful servants."

Kizzy said, "See, I told you he'd get it right."

Cassie said, "I'm glad he said that our decisions about faith come as we are facing a host of new and puzzling challenges. That's the question we have been making in the campaign. Who's in charge of the germline: Man or God?"

Carson said, "It's time to watch YouTube. Andrea Bocelli is doing a special Easter program from the Duomo in Milan."

35

Onward

The camera meandered slowly toward the altar of the cavernous Duomo cathedral. Streams of light peeped entered through stained-glass windows past rows of empty pews. A man, tiny in the distance, stood alone at the altar, next to an enormous pipe organ.

The great tenor Andrea Bocelli, elegant in his tuxedo, was about to sing for the world, having explained earlier why he wanted to sing. "I believe in the strength of praying together; I believe in the Christian Easter, a universal symbol of rebirth that everyone—whether they are believers or not – truly needs right now."

As the camera neared Bocelli—close enough to see his closed eyes—the organist Emanuele Vianelli began to play. It was a rare moment, an Easter Sunday for the ages. And when he sang the haunting verses of "Ave Maria" the music rose above the troubles of the world.

Bocelli was delivering God's message of love, healing and hope to Italy and the rest of the world during a most difficult time.

The scene shifted to the front steps of the Duomo for his last song, "Amazing Grace." And there, beneath a beautiful blue sky, Bocelli—blinded at age 12—sang from the heart: "Amazing grace! How sweet the sound, that saved a wretch like me. I once was lost, but now am found; was blind, but now I see."

Kizzy cried throughout, her head resting on Cassie's shoulder. Carson and Cassie broke down too when Bocelli sang "Was blind, but now I see."

When it was over, Kizzy said, "God used a blind man, singing in an empty church to give us peace." She sat straight up. "But to have hope and get the peace we have to trust and obey."

Cassie hugged her. "Happy Easter, Kizzy."

Carson said, "The worst of times can sometimes be the best of times."

"Amen." Cassie looked at Kizzy. "The message of resurrection gives us hope, but it's like you said: 'We have to trust and obey.'"

"But trust in who? Trust in what?" Carson said.

Kizzy said, "Trust in God, and live like he wants us to. The rest will take care of itself."

"I hope that means I will win my race for Congress." Cassie smiled.

"It's not about winning, Cassie," Kizzy said. "It's about fighting the good fight and leaving the outcome to God. Remember this: I didn't win when they put me on trial for killing Cormac. It was a hung jury. But the fight we fought was what put Bully Bigshot in prison and put the Eugenics Center out of business."

Carson smiled. "I get it. If Cassie keeps fighting, She'll put TASAR and the transhumanists out of business. Even if she doesn't win a seat in Congress."

Kizzy said, "Fighting the good fight has always worked for me. It's a lesson I learned a long time ago from Uncle Mac."

Carson said, "That gives me an idea for another video. It's about the audacity and hubris of people who think they can do a better job than God."

Cassie frowned. "This is Easter, Carson. Let's give politics a rest."

***

Later that afternoon, they sat in Kizzy's backyard debating the pros and cons of all the rules that had been put in place by government. Eventually Cassie posed a most important question to Carson. "Will St. James Prep open on schedule?"

"Who knows?" Carson said. "This virus has got everything screwed up."

They talked about St. James for a while longer, but Kizzy was not listening. She was thumbing through her Bible and humming "Onward Christian Soldiers."

"What are you looking for, Kizzy?" Cassie said.

"I found it." She leaned back and looked at Cassie.

"Bocelli's singing got me to thinking about the timing of all this: Easter Sunday, empty churches, people separated, scared, and worried sick.

"It's a time for truth. A time to decide. It's the question you've been raising about the strange new world. Who's in charge? Are we going to stick with God or are we going to go with man?"

Cassie said, "It's an age-old question."

Kizzy nodded yes, then pointed to a verse in the Bible.

"Read Ezekiel 33:10. It's *the* question the people of God asked when they were in exile and despair."

Cassie smiled at Kizzy then read the question aloud.

"How should we then live?"

ACKNOWLEDGMENTS

Writing at age 84 is harder than it used to be.

But so is everything else.

A Pearl for Kizzy ended with a scene that contemplated the atomic bombing of Hiroshima and Nagasaki in 1945. Since then much has changed. Man has gone to the moon, jet airplanes criss-cross the world, people live longer. I could go on and on, but we have digested these changes, epic as they are.

The changes in technology, genetic engineering, and artificial intelligence are of a different sort. They are explosive, outracing the imagination. Moore's Law—an observation made in 1965—postulates that the speed and capability of our computers doubles every couple of years.

These changes occur exponentially. We cannot digest them as easily as we have other changes because we are being force-fed. Consider for example the ubiquitous cellphones and how quickly the new models and constant updates change our lives.

Once I decided to write this sequel—*The Thinking Spot*—I had to relearn biology and study the technological changes that are occurring at warp speed.

I did not presume to write as a scientific expert. My goal was to learn enough to write a story that would frame the fundamental issues humanity will face as we grapple with the avalanche of new technology, artificial intelligence, and genetic engineering.

I have tried to write in a way that can be easily read and understood, satisfied that readers—if provoked—can find a world of research material online, as I did.

To provoke debate I presented my protagonist, Cassie, as one who begins her life journey as a secular humanist but winds up with a Christian worldview. All too often the reverse is true in this modern era.

Dearborn College near Philadelphia is fictional. So is Montmartre Law School in Rhode Island. I used imaginary schools to avoid preconceived notions about the kind of learning a student might receive at one of our many fine institutions.

Finally, this is the place to give thanks to my beta-readers.

John Sennett, a retired FBI Agent who I met when he served as president of the FBI Agents Association; Captain Benjamin Steiger (USMC), the son of Fritz Steiger, my campaign manager when I ran for the U. S. Senate; my son, Lt. Commander Sam Bethune (USN, Retired) who has read all my work and is a trusted advisor; Dr. Larry Killough, a longtime friend who is a member of my Sunday School Class in Searcy, Arkansas; Sheila Anthony, a wise woman, lawyer and longtime friend who is also my son's mother-in-law.

Three of my eight granddaughters: Nicole Winters, a graduate of Mary Washington University who creates and markets extraordinary ceramic pieces; Bailey Nassetta, an artistic graduate of New York University's Tisch School of Experimental Theater; and Mason Nassetta, a graduate of the University of Virginia, who began her career at Live Nation in Los Angeles but now lives in Nashville, Tennessee.

My friend, Karen Martin, the talented senior editor of the Perspective section of the *Arkansas Democrat-Gazette*, copyedited *A Pearl for Kizzy* in 2016. As I neared the end of the manuscript for this sequel, *The Thinking Place*, I asked her to help me again. She makes the hard business of editing seem like fun, and that is not easy to do. She is a delightful woman who encourages me and makes valuable suggestions as we work to produce a presentable piece of literature.

My beloved wife of 61 years, Lana, is an extraordinary person. She has been at my side through thick and thin, highs and lows, successes, and failures. Her counsel as an English teacher is invaluable. But she has unique characteristics that endear her to people, especially me: She loves without qualification, is upbeat, and refuses always to let anything get her down.

Made in the USA
Columbia, SC
12 June 2020